This book belongs to:

. . . .

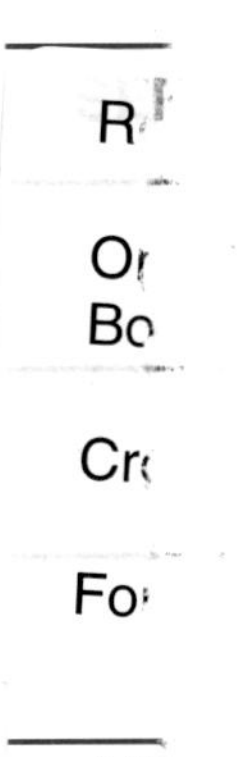

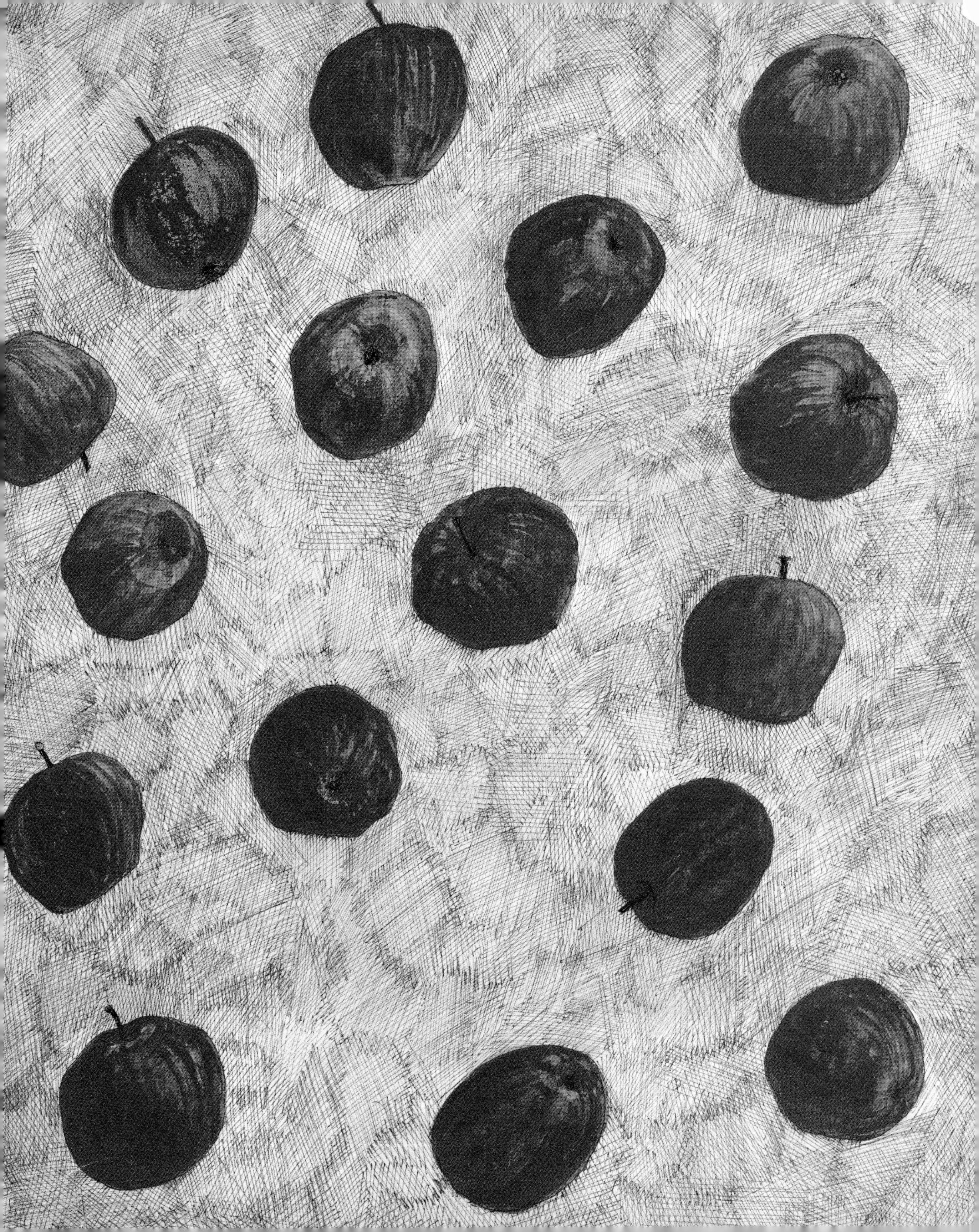

To the memory of Max Velthuijs, the master.

First published in Great Britain in 2006 by Andersen Press Ltd., 20 Vauxhall Bridge Road, London SW1V 2SA.
This paperback edition first published in 2008 by Andersen Press Ltd.
Published in Australia by Random House Australia Pty., Level 3, 100 Pacific Highway, North Sydney, NSW 2060.
 Colour separated in Switzerland by Photolitho AG, Zürich.
Printed and bound in Singapore.

10 9 8 7 6 5 4 3 2 1

British Library Cataloguing in Publication Data available.

ISBN 978 1 84270 593 3

This book has been printed on acid-free paper

Andersen Press • London

"This is fun," thought Ringo Rabbit. "And it's something that nobody else can do." He was juggling four red apples at the time. As he juggled, he hummed a little tune.

Just then Rubens Pig arrived.

“That’s fun, isn’t it?” said Rubens. “I can do it too. Look!”

Ringo stopped humming. “But I thought that I was the only one who could do it,” he said.

“Fancy that,” said Rubens. “Mary Sheep taught me. Come on, let’s go and see her.”

"Cooee! Mary!" called Rubens. "Ringo thought he was the only one who could juggle four red apples. Go on, show him."

Mary juggled. "I was k-k-kindly shown how to d-do it by B-B-Bono D-D-Dog," she stuttered. "I f-find it such f-f-fun. P-P-Perhaps we should v-visit him."

"How nice to see you all," Bono greeted them. "Sit down and have a glass of orange while I juggle four red apples, just for fun."

"R-R-Ringo thought only he c-c-could do it," said Mary.

Bono chuckled and stopped juggling. "Up you get," he said. "We're going over to Kiki Cat's place. I learned it from her."

"Silly old me thinking that I was the only one who could juggle four red apples," Ringo said to himself.

"There's Rubens and Mary and Bono: that already makes four of us. If Kiki can do it that will make five."

Kiki was actually juggling four red apples when they arrived. They sat and watched her. "There, what did I tell you?" said Bono. Then to Kiki he said, "Ringo thought he was the only one who could do that."

"Oh cool," purred Kiki. "Follow me. I'll take you to the expert who taught me, Stevie Frog."

"Yoho, Stevie," called Kiki. "Poor old Ringo thought he was the only one who could juggle four red apples."

Stevie laughed and juggled.

"It's great fun, isn't it?" said Stevie. "Dee Dee Duck showed me how to do it. Hop aboard, I'll take you to her."

"Good day, Dee Dee. We've come to see you juggle four red apples." Stevie laughed. "Ringo thought he was the only one that could do it."

Dee Dee juggled.

"You know, it's rather fun," she said. "I was lucky enough to be trained by the Honourable Edgar Fox. Now smarten yourselves up, we'll go and pay him our respects."

"What a funny old world," sighed Ringo. "There I was thinking that I was the only one who could juggle four red apples . . .

Then what do I find? All my friends can do it. There's Rubens, Mary, Bono, Kiki, Stevie and Dee Dee. And if Edgar can do it, then everyone can do it."

"I say, what? Can I juggle four red apples?" said Edgar. "I should jolly well think so! Here we go. Now this I call fun. What?"

"Ringo thought only he could do it," said Dee Dee.

"I say, really?" said Edgar. "But Ringo Old Thing, have you forgotten? It was you who taught me?"

"Oh yes, so I did, I had forgotten," said Ringo.

Everyone laughed, especially Ringo.

Rubens suddenly asked, “Ringo, tell us, who taught you?”
“I taught myself,” said Ringo.
“So actually it’s thanks to you that we can all do it,” said Dee Dee. “Thank you, Ringo.”
“Thank you, Ringo,” the others echoed.

Ringo blushed. "Oh, stop being mushy," he said. "Let's juggle."
So juggle they did.

"Who cares if I'm not the only one who can do it," thought Ringo. "It's much more fun all doing it together."

Other books by

David McKee

Charlotte's Piggy Bank

Elmer

George's Invisible Watch

Isabel's Noisy Tummy

Mr Benn, Gladiator

Not Now, Bernard

The Conquerors

Three Monsters

Two Can Toucan

Tusk Tusk

Human Resources

Contents

Outline

Businesses are made up of people. Irrespective of job title, age, sex, race, length of service, importance or seniority, the common factor is that they are all people. People bring to a business more than their knowledge, expertise, experience and skills. They each bring ideas, knowledge, intelligence, an ability to think and a range of experiences as employees, citizens, shoppers, neighbours and, perhaps, parents. They bring energy, personality, humour, enthusiasm, expectations, temperament, values and beliefs.

No two people are the same and no other resource offers such a variety of gifts in such a small package – not even the microchip. It is the contribution of each individual, added to the contributions of all the other individuals in the business, that determines whether the business is successful and whether it survives or not.

Getting the right person in the right job, and giving her or him the facilities and support to do the job willingly to the required standards, is a key concern for every business. This unit examines this important topic.

Note: each of the Collins Educational Advanced GNVQ Business Units have been published separately. Figures have been numbered according to the Unit in which they appear.

Published by
Collins Educational Ltd
An imprint of HarperCollins *Publishers*
77–85 Fulham Palace Road
Hammersmith
London W6 8JB

First published 1996

ISBN 0–00–322450–3

Series commissioned by Richard Jackman.
Designed and edited by DSM Partnership.
Cover designed by Trevor Burrows.
Cartoons by Daniel Betts.
Interview simulation designed by Lucy Gunn BSc, MSc, MBPS © 1995.
Project managed by Kay Wright.
Production by Jane Bressloff.
Printed and bound by Scotprint Ltd., Musselburgh, Scotland.

Acknowledgements

The authors and publisher would like to thank the following for permission to reproduce material:

Bally Shoe Factories, Norwich, photograph (p. 20); *Daily Telegraph*: 'Union to sue insurance firm over bullying boss', by Hugh Gurdon and Ben Fenton, 13 September 1995 (p. 9); 'Ambulance controller loses unfair sacking fight', 23 September 1995 (p. 12); '£30,000 damages for Irish insult' by Nigel Bunyan, 23 September 1995 (p. 14); 'Ford factories back to normal', 18 November 1995 (p. 16); 'Judges dash hopes of backdated dismissal claims', by Terence Shaw, 27 January 1996; Design to Distribution Limited, photograph (p. 20); Department of Trade and Industry, Application to an industrial tribunal, (p. 17); *Financial Times*, 'Employers "must take care" on job references', 8 July 1995; The *Guardian*, 'ITN union staff vote to strike', by Andrew Culf, 24 January 1996 (p. 16); Independent on Sunday, 'Personnel officers are a waste of time, says new study', 15 May 1994 (p. 31); Motorola advetisement (p. 47); Whitbread plc, advertisement (p. 47).

Every effort has been made to contact copyright holders, but if any have been inadvertently overlooked, the publishers will be pleased to make the necessary arrangements at the first opportunity.

Investigate human resourcing

RIGHTS OF EMPLOYERS AND EMPLOYEES

The rights of employers and employees – the legal relationship between them – rests solely on the **contract of employment**. A contract is an agreement between two parties. The essence is agreement.

CONTRACT OF EMPLOYMENT

A contract of employment is an agreement between an employer and an employee. It sets out the basis on which the employee carries out the legitimate work of the employer in return for the payment of wages.

The contract of employment is not a single, written document such as one might find in the sort of commercial transaction you consider in the activity below. It is a complicated combination of both **express** and **implied** terms, and may be **verbal** as well as **written**. (An exception is an apprenticeship contract; this must be in writing.) We will examine the nature of the contract by first looking at express terms and then the implied terms, including some statutory rights.

ACTIVITY

1 Look up the meaning of the noun 'contract' in a good dictionary. Write it down in your notes.

2 Now see how many contracts (written or verbal) you can identify in your own everyday life. Make a list of five or more. There are probably dozens. For example, if your television is rented, then a contract exists between someone and the television rental company. Similarly, contracts cover mortgages, the supply of gas and electricity to your home, the telephone service, and so on.

3 Ask to see some actual contract documents if you can. Can you identify a common theme in all contracts? Why do you think they are so complicated and written in such difficult language?

4 Are there any contracts you personally are a party to? For example, think of your relationship with your school or college; think of buying or selling an item or think of renting something, such as a flat or a video. In any contract, what are your obligations? Make some notes which you can use to help you understand one contract that you will (hopefully) have soon – a contract of employment.

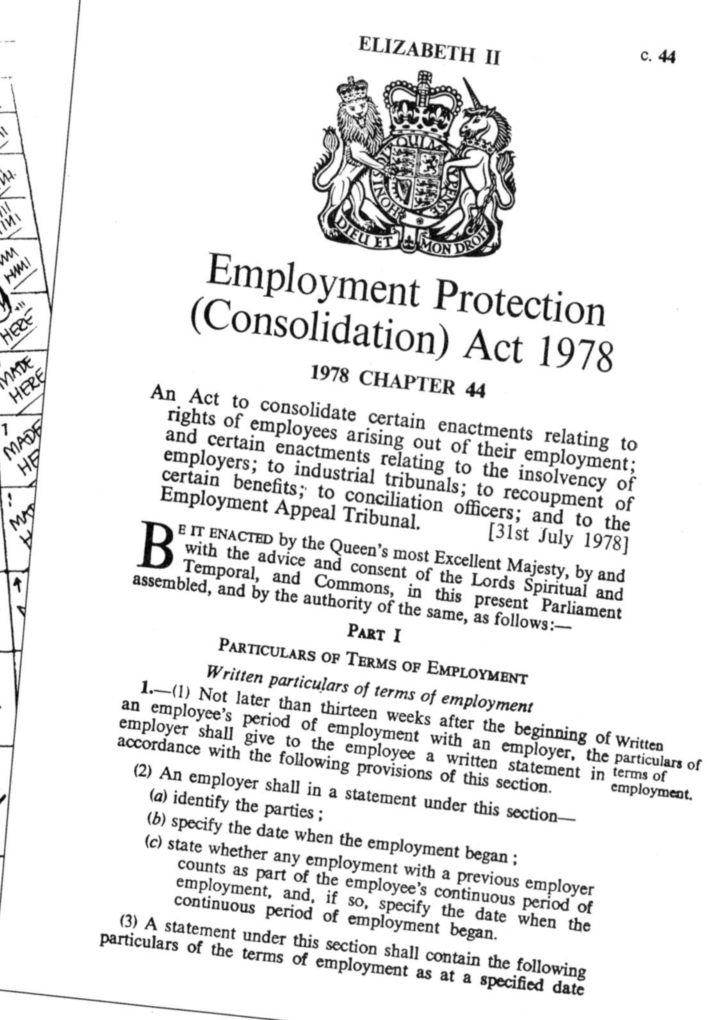

ELIZABETH II c. 44 1

DIEU ET MON DROIT

Employment Protection (Consolidation) Act 1978

1978 CHAPTER 44

An Act to consolidate certain enactments relating to rights of employees arising out of their employment; and certain enactments relating to the insolvency of employers; to industrial tribunals; to recoupment of certain benefits; to conciliation officers; and to the Employment Appeal Tribunal. [31st July 1978]

BE IT ENACTED by the Queen's most Excellent Majesty, by and with the advice and consent of the Lords Spiritual and Temporal, and Commons, in this present Parliament assembled, and by the authority of the same, as follows:—

PART I

PARTICULARS OF TERMS OF EMPLOYMENT

Written particulars of terms of employment

1.—(1) Not later than thirteen weeks after the beginning of an employee's period of employment with an employer, the employer shall give to the employee a written statement in accordance with the following provisions of this section.

Written particulars of terms of employment.

(2) An employer shall in a statement under this section—

(*a*) identify the parties;

(*b*) specify the date when the employment began;

(*c*) state whether any employment with a previous employer counts as part of the employee's continuous period of employment, and, if so, specify the date when the continuous period of employment began.

(3) A statement under this section shall contain the following particulars of the terms of employment as at a specified date

FIGURE 4.1: Extract from the Employment Protection (Consolidation) Act 1978.

EXPRESS TERMS

Express terms are stated plainly, exactly, and unmistakably during the making of the agreement. Usually a **letter of appointment** is given to a new employee. This is a very important document because it sets out the details of the agreement between the two parties in writing, and it is usually accepted in writing. The letter of appointment becomes the cornerstone of the contract and may be called upon in the event of a dispute between the employer and employee about the nature of the agreement.

In the event that a verbal offer is made, and a verbal acceptance is given, the agreement is based upon what was said during the interview and what was agreed during any discussions between the employer and prospective employee. Any additional detail about what the job entails – such as a **job description**, **work rules** or **employee handbook** – may also be called upon to clarify the details of the contract. So what is written, and anything that is said which the two parties intend to be binding upon them, is part of the contract of employment.

Fundamental rights of employees were first set out in statute law in 1963 and 1971. (Statute law is law enacted by Parliament and is the highest law in the land.) In 1978 the law was amended by the **Employment Protection (Consolidation) Act**. This gives employees the right to receive written particulars of the terms of employment.

Under this Act, most employees are entitled to receive a written statement of the main terms and conditions of their employment within thirteen weeks of starting work (see *Fig.4.1*). In April 1993, a European Union directive reduced this time period to eight weeks.

The written statement must include:

- **the employer's and the employee's names;**
- **the date upon which employment began, including any previous employment that is to be considered continuous;**
- **the job title;**
- **the payment scale or rate and the frequency of payment;**
- **hours of work;**
- **holiday entitlement and holiday pay;**
- **sick pay and allowances;**
- **pension schemes;**
- **the amount of notice to end the contract;**
- **disciplinary and appeal procedures, and grievance procedures.**

ACTIVITY

1. **Ask the librarian in your school or college library, or in your local public library, for a copy of the Employment Protection (Consolidation) Act 1978.**
2. **These Acts are not as difficult to follow as you may think. Turn to the first page – it is a type of index which describes the 'arrangement of sections'. What does it say about Section 1?**
3. **Now turn to Section 1 and read it. You can see where the list of items that must be included in a written statement comes from.**
4. **Return to the arrangement of sections again. There are nine 'Parts'. List the title of each part in your notes – you can ignore Part IX. Note the extent of the Act, that is, all the things it covers.**

If an employer fails to provide a written statement of the main terms and conditions of employment, an employee could exercise his or her legal right to ask an industrial tribunal to decide what ought to have been in the written statement. This is then imposed upon the employer. Hardly a way to begin a mutually satisfactory and productive relationship! The employer (if there are more than twenty employees) is also obliged to ensure that every employee has a copy of the disciplinary and grievance procedure or access to it.

IMPLIED TERMS

If you think about the many eventualities that could occur in the relationship between an employer and an employee, it is probably impossible to predict them all, or to put them in a form that could be scrutinised and agreed by both parties. To overcome the difficulties that this complexity creates, the courts will read into contracts **implied terms** that are necessary to allow the contract to work.

Some implied terms are reasonably straightforward. For example, all contracts of employment will be deemed to include common law duties, such as the duty of care (safety); each party has a duty not to jeopardise the safety of the other.

Employees also have a common law duty of obedience. The duty of obedience (although modified by both UK statute laws and European Union laws and regulations) remains fundamental to employment relationships. If an order given by a supervisor is within the contractual authority of the employer, the employee has an obligation to obey or run the risk of losing his or her job.

Other implied terms are less clear. In those cases we must look to the courts to give direction. In the case *Shell UK Ltd v Lostock Garage Ltd 1976*, Lord Denning – then Master of the Rolls – suggested the test as to whether an implied term is to be read in, should be: 'has the law already defined the obligation or the extent of it? If so, let it be followed. If not, look to see what would be **reasonable** in the **general run** of such cases, and then say what the obligation shall be.' (The added emphasis is the author's.)

The obligation in such a case would be an implied term. Can you imagine the difficulties this creates in trying to decide whether an employer or an employee is in breach of an implied term in the contract? It is probably beyond the average manager or employee. It would require a lawyer to examine case law and advise the firm or individual. Case law is based on decisions given by a judge in one case, which then become guidance in all other similar cases.

As a general guide, however, there will be implied terms in all contracts relating to the following:

- a duty to act with good faith towards the employer;
- a duty of care, each party for the other;
- a duty to maintain confidence and trust between the employer and the employee;
- a duty of the employer to provide work, and a duty of the employee to carry it out conscientiously;
- a duty of the employer to give reasonable support to all employees so that they can carry out their work;
- similarly, the employer has a duty to support its managers in their managerial duties.

Have you noticed that where people have **rights**, they also have **duties** or **obligations**? It is impossible to separate them.

- **If you have a *right* to an education, you have a *duty* to attend and to learn within your ability.**
- **If your teacher has a *right* to your attention, she or he has a *duty* to make the material relevant and interesting to you.**

ACTIVITY

In a group of three or four colleagues, consider other situations in which rights have duties attached to them. Look at situations relating to education, employment, sports, social life, the environment, civil liberties, equal opportunities, and anything else you wish.

1 List the rights and associated duties.

2 What conclusions can you draw from your list about 'the nature of justice?

There are some contracts into which particular implied terms are read. For example, a skilled craftsperson would be expected to know his or her craft and to practise it to an acceptable standard of quality and safety. This not only applies to crafts but to professional people as well. For example, teachers would be expected to know their subjects and how to communicate them to students in an acceptable fashion.

Some firms also negotiate agreements with trade unions. These **collective agreements** usually relate to wages and conditions of work. For example, a teacher's salary might be agreed between the employer and the National Union of Teachers during the annual pay negotiations. These agreements are not legally binding between the firm and union but, once they are incorporated into an employee's contract of employment, they are binding upon both the employer and the employee.

Finally, there may be occasions when **'custom and practice'** is considered to be an implied term in the contract. Custom and practice is the term given to unofficial working practices operated by the workforce which are not covered by a specific rule or procedure. They are condoned by management but have never been 'agreed' by management.

Custom and practice is hard to establish and courts tend not to be sympathetic to arguments that it constitutes an implied term of contract. However, if a custom or a practice is *reasonable*, if it is *certain* and if it is *well known*, then it may be deemed part of the contract.

Once again, in cases like this, we must look to the courts for guidance. The case *Devonald v Rosser 1906* gives us a precedent: 'a custom so universal that no workman could be supposed to have entered into this service without looking to it as part of the contract'. Although ninety years old, this judgement is still used to help decide whether something is custom and practice or not.

STATUTORY RIGHTS

In order to clarify matters, and to ensure that employee rights are protected from abuse by powerful employers, Parliament has passed numerous employment laws in the past thirty years. It is not possible to waive these rights, so they are read into (or implied in) the contract of employment of all employees in the land.

The main Acts of Parliament that relate to employment are:

- **Equal Pay Act 1970;**
- **Fair Employment (NI) Act;**
- **Health and Safety at Work Act 1974;**
- **Sex Discrimination Act 1975;**
- **Race Relations Act 1976;**
- **Employment Protection (Consolidation) Act 1978;**
- **Employment Act(s) 1980 to 1990.**

These Acts provide rights to employees. Some rights are dependent on length of service; for example, you may have to be an employee for two years before some rights apply. The main rights conferred by these Acts are:

- **not to be discriminated against on grounds of race, sex or marriage;**
- **to receive equal pay for work of equal worth;**
- **to receive a written statement of the main terms of the contract;**
- **to be a member of a union or not, as the individual wishes;**
- **to receive notice of termination of employment;**
- **to be paid redundancy payments depending upon age and length of service;**
- **to work in safe and healthy conditions;**
- **to receive sick pay;**
- **not to be unfairly dismissed;**
- **to be given a written reason for dismissal.**

ACTIVITY

Look through the list of employee rights enshrined in law. If these are respected honestly by all employers, would we have a fair and just system of employment?

What other rights do you think should be included, if any?

If your 'other rights' are made statutory requirements, what effect might they have on the prosperity of the business?

Note that UK employment law is being amended or supplemented to meet European Union (EU) regulations and directives. Business managers must now take into account European laws and directives.

To summarise, a contract of employment is made up of many parts:

- **the offer and acceptance of the job;**
- **the written statement of the terms and conditions;**
- **any other written and agreed documents;**
- **common law duties and rights;**
- **other implied terms;**
- **collective agreements;**
- **custom and practice;**
- **UK and EU statutory rights.**

Collectively, this has an impact on business in that the contract of employment gives both employers and employees rights and confers duties, one to the other. The notion of 'British justice' applies as much in the workplace as in any other walk of life.

The average manager and employee does not usually have a detailed knowledge of law. So, they need some sort of structure to work within – and some set of procedures to guide them.

Discipline and grievance procedures

Every employee in companies employing more than twenty people is entitled to receive (or have available) a copy of the company's disciplinary and grievance procedure within eight weeks of joining the company. The fact that the law is so specific indicates the importance of a system of justice for both employer and employees within every place of work.

It is the legal responsibility of the employer to prepare the disciplinary and grievance procedures. If trade unions are recognised, they will doubtless want a say in the structure and content of the procedures.

ACTIVITY

1. **Using a good dictionary, look up the meanings of discipline and grievance. Write these definitions in your notes, and study them so that you could explain them to any of your colleagues without reference to your notes.**
2. **Now get copies of your school or college's disciplinary and grievance procedures for students. Study the procedures and understand how they work. Discuss them with your teacher if you wish.**
3. **Prepare a short presentation (to last five minutes) in which you explain the system of justice in your school or college. Comment on the advantages of having such a process compared with not having one.**

Procedure for discipline

Discipline can be defined as 'a system of rules for behaviour'. Disciplinary action, then, is taken against people who do not follow those rules.

The Advisory, Conciliation and Arbitration Service (ACAS) has produced a code of practice – *Disciplinary Practice and Procedures in Employment* – to act as a guide to those preparing procedures. It is not a legal requirement to follow the code, but employers would be expected to conform to the spirit of the code.

The essence of this procedure is 'fairness':

- **fair and equal treatment of all individuals;**
- **fair methods of dealing with people;**
- **fair standards of work that apply to all jobs;**
- **fair expectations – people know what is expected of them;**
- **fair decisions – all people are treated similarly and decisions are based only on the facts;**
- **fair outcomes – the right of appeal is given to people who have sensible grounds for disagreeing with the decision.**

Managers should be concerned with discipline all the time, not just when someone breaks the rules. They should be monitoring the behaviour of employees in three areas – **attendance**, **performance** and **co-operation** – and taking minor corrective action all the time. This action may, for example, take the form of additional training or counselling; its purpose is to ensure that people are giving of their best. If one or two people are allowed to get away with things that result in other people having to do their work or cover for them, morale is likely to suffer. Good, fair, consistent discipline is important in building high morale.

If minor corrective action fails to change an employee's unacceptable behaviour or performance, a manager might decide to invoke the disciplinary procedure. If the evidence justifies it, the manager may decide to begin disciplinary action against the offender. Always, however, the actions must be in accordance with the company's stated procedure. This usually includes:

- **one verbal warning;**
- **a first written warning;**
- **a final written warning;**
- **if these fail to correct the unacceptable behaviour or performance, then the person may be dismissed.**

Because employees being disciplined may feel under pressure, and consequently might be unable to give a good account of themselves, they are entitled to bring a trade union official or a colleague along. Disciplinary action can last weeks or months. Throughout its duration, employers must provide the support and training needed to correct the behaviour.

If an employee commits an act of **gross misconduct**, he or she may be dismissed without warning or notice – this is termed **'summary dismissal'** in consequence of gross misconduct. Matters that may be considered gross misconduct should be specified in the procedure. Examples of gross misconduct might include failure to obey an instruction, fighting, dangerous practices, drunkenness, drugs abuse, theft or other dishonesty.

The following article gives an example of the use of disciplinary and grievance procedures.

Union to sue insurance firm over bullying boss

A trade union is planning legal action against a leading insurance company over alleged corporate bullying. The case could force hostile managers to pay compensation to their staff.

The Manufacturing, Science and Finance Union said yesterday that its lawyers were preparing a case against the Co-operative Insurance Society and one of its managers on behalf of an employee who has been on sick leave for five months with a stress-related illness.

The case is believed to be one of the first of its kind, although lawyers have been saying for months that legislation introduced to conform with European law would lead to a flood of claims. The CIS case centres on the actions of one manager in a claims office in the Midlands. He is alleged to have verbally abused and mistreated all his staff for more than two years.

Bill Hamilton, a spokesman for the union, said: 'It's not just a question of employers providing machinery that is in good safe working order. They should also provide rational bosses who can treat their staff with reason rather than ranting and raving throughout the working week.'

But the company said that the manager concerned had already been subject to 'strong disciplinary action' under the normal grievance procedure, although he still worked in the same office as a manager.

A spokesman said: 'The staff concerned have been given an assurance that any repeat of the manager's unacceptable behaviour will not be tolerated.'

Daily Telegraph,
13 September 1995

Appeals

Anyone who feels that they have been unfairly disciplined has a right of appeal. The appeal should be to a different manager than the one who undertook the disciplinary action. This should be specified in the procedure; it is usually a senior manager. The appeal should be heard quickly after the event – three days seems reasonable. All the facts of the case should be put before the senior manager, and he or she should consider them impartially. Usually, the senior manager's decision is final.

Procedure for grievances

Every employer, irrespective of the size of the business, must provide employees with details of the **grievance procedure**. Grievances should be distinguished from common grumbles about pay or the boss. Grievances relate to aspects of the contract of employment that an individual or group feels are being breached by the employer. It may be about pay or bonuses, the way the supervisor treats people, discrimination of one sort or another, or any other genuine concern felt by an employee.

It is quite difficult for an employee to bring a complaint against the boss, or the organisation generally. Besides the impact it may have on future relationships, the employee may not want to rock the boat. This is a case where it can be helpful to be a member of a trade union, so that it can represent you.

But it is important that an organisation should care about feelings of injustice felt by its employees. Loyalty and harmony are unlikely to grow in an uncaring culture. So providing them with the means of securing justice is good motivational policy. As with discipline, managers should be sensing grievances and dealing with them before they can cause any lasting harm to relationships.

A grievance procedure should provide people with the assurance that grievances can be brought into the open, and that they will be dealt with professionally, without rancour or reprisal. Good managers should encourage this openness – because the alternative, a discontented staff, is not in the organisation's best interest.

A formal grievance procedure may have three stages.

- **First**, a person with a grievance should take it up with his or her immediate manager and discuss it with a view to resolving the issue quickly. Usually three days is considered sufficient at this first stage.

- **Second**, if it is not resolved to the complainant's satisfaction, it is passed in writing to the next level manager, who should deal with it within five days. The complainant can seek help from a colleague if needed.

- **Third**, if it is not resolved, a senior manager, probably at director level, will meet the complainant and any other people involved and make a final decision, based on the facts of the case. Again, this should be within five days.

In settling grievances satisfactorily, a company is signalling its concern for justice. If its procedure is perceived as fair, it will be accepted and used.

Dismissal

Every contract of employment comes to an end. It may be because the contract is for a specific term and the term has ended; the employee may have reached retirement age or he or she may have found another job and resigned. Alternatively, the employer may terminate the contract of employment with or without the employee's agreement.

The Employment Protection (Consolidation) Act sets out reasons for dismissal that are fair in law. They are:

- **capability;**
- **ill health;**
- **conduct;**
- **some other substantial reason;**
- **redundancy.**

Capability

If an employee fails to do the job to the standard required because of lack of ability or skill, the employer can invoke the disciplinary procedure described opposite. After a reasonable amount of training and support, if the standard is still not achieved, the employee can be dismissed.

Ill health

This is a sensitive issue and needs careful handling. If a person suffers a long-term illness that keeps him or her off work, and the job must be filled, the employer should go through a process of careful consultation with the employee and medical advisors and, if a return to work is unlikely in a reasonable time, the employer may dismiss the employee. In such a case, the employer must give the employee the statutory notice and pay full wages during the period of notice, whether sick pay is being received or not.

Conduct

A disciplinary procedure should define gross misconduct and set out the process for establishing whether misconduct has taken place. It is fair for an employer to dismiss an employee for gross misconduct without notice, and without pay in lieu of notice. For ordinary misconduct, such as persistent lateness, it will be fair to dismiss an employee if the disciplinary procedure has been used to its full extent.

Some other substantial reason

It would be impossible to list all the reasons that would be 'fair' in all circumstances. An industrial tribunal has power to decide what constitutes a substantial reason for dismissal.

For example, if, in order to protect its business, an organisation needs to make some essential changes to an employee's contract and that employee will not accept them, it may be fair to dismiss. Every effort should be made to persuade the employee of the necessity to accept the changes but, if this fails, the employer has little option but to dismiss the employee.

Another example is when an employee is closely associated with a person who is in serious competition with the employee's organisation. If the employee could pass on information that would damage his or her employer, then it is probably fair to dismiss.

Redundancy

People are not redundant – jobs are redundant. The sad thing is that if the job disappears, and there is no other appropriate work for the jobholder, he or she has to be dismissed. Redundancy occurs if the employer ceases the business in which the employee is working, or if a particular kind of work is reduced or ceases.

The resulting dismissal is fair if the people to be made redundant are chosen according to agreed redundancy criteria. Seeking volunteers for redundancy or adopting a 'last in, first out' policy are often used, but both of these approaches can create an imbalance in the remaining staff. Selecting people to be made redundant by levels of performance, by attendance levels, or by some other criteria is only fair if the people who may be affected are aware of the criteria.

Alternative work must be found if possible. If another person is being appointed to a job that the redundant person could have done, then the redundancy is unfair.

Recognised trade unions must be informed in writing and consulted about any redundancies. The employer has to inform them of plans for redundancies, and listen to their comments and advice – but there is no obligation to act on this advice. For large-scale redundancies, an employer must give notice to both the Department for Education and Employment and the unions. An employer must give thirty day's notice if planning to make between ten and a hundred redundancies; if more than a hundred redundancies are planned, ninety day's notice must be given.

Many companies have redundancy agreements with recognised unions. Minimum redundancy payments are set by law, but unions will try to get a better deal for their members. The calculation is based upon age and length of service. For any employee over eighteen and having at least two year's service with the employer, the statutory minimum payments are based on the following formula:

- **half a week's pay for every year's service between the ages of 18 and 22;**
- **one week's pay for every year's service between the ages of 23 and 41;**
- **one-and-a-half week's pay for every year between the ages of 42 and 64.**

The Department for Education and Employment sets an upper limit for redundancy payments. In January 1996, the upper limit for redundancy pay was £210 per week. If an employee earns more than this upper limit, the employer is only required to apply the formula for statutory redundancy pay to £210 of the weekly earnings.

ACTIVITY

Calculate the statutory redundancy pay that would be due in each of the following cases:

(a) a person aged 21, with 3 years service, currently earning £125 per week;

(b) a person aged 43, with 20 years service, currently earning £207 per week;

(c) a person aged 61, with 14 years service, currently earning £384 per week.

Remember to take into account the maximum upper limit for redundancy pay.

Ambulance controller loses unfair sacking fight

An ambulance controller sacked for cancelling a trip to a dying 16-year-old girl lost his claim for unfair dismissal yesterday.

An industrial tribunal in Exeter heard that the girl's father had twice dialled 999 when his daughter collapsed at their home in St Austell, Cornwall, two years ago.

After being told that the journey could not be authorised until the case was checked with their family doctor, the father took his daughter to hospital himself.

The daughter died weeks later although a post-mortem showed that the delay in reaching hospital had not contributed to her death.

During the three-day hearing, the man who sacked the controller denounced him as a liar and said public confidence in the service would be damaged if the controller kept his job.

Ken Wenman, West Country Ambulance Service Trust director, said there should have been no quibbling over calls. He said a record card noting the father's final call appeared to have been doctored.

Daily Telegraph, 23 September 1995

UNFAIR DISMISSAL

People who have been employed by an employer for two years have a legal right not to be unfairly dismissed. Any reason for dismissal not listed above may be unfair. For example, the following do not constitute grounds for dismissal:

- **membership or non-membership of a trade union;**
- **pregnancy;**
- **sex or race (or creed or political affiliation in Northern Ireland);**
- **a spent conviction under the Rehabilitation of Offenders Act 1974.**

Not only does the *reason* for dismissal have to be fair, the *method* of the dismissal must also be fair. Someone might be dismissed for a fair reason under the Employment Protection (Consolidation) Act, but claim unfair dismissal because the method of the dismissal was unfair.

A person who wants to claim unfair dismissal must do so to an industrial tribunal within three months of being dismissed. The **Advisory, Conciliation and Arbitration Service (ACAS)** will be asked to try to conciliate, but if a settlement is not reached, the case will go to **industrial tribunal**. The role of industrial tribunals and ACAS is discussed in more detail later in this element.

ACTIVITY

Read the article above about the dismissal of the ambulance controller. Which 'fair reason' would cover this dismissal?

Imagine you are the manager who received the complaint from the girl's father. You have to plan how to handle it so as to be fair to each party. Describe the steps you should take to ensure that the decision you make is in accordance with the procedure and is fair.

It is not necessary to write an essay – you can draw a step-by-step flow diagram to illustrate the process if you prefer.

Constructive Dismissal

There are cases when the employer takes actions or behaves in such a way that an employee feels it is impossible to continue working and walks out.

Examples would be where:

- **an employer does not provide safe working conditions – expecting a worker to use a grinding wheel without providing proper training and without protective equipment;**
- **a senior manager keeps overruling a supervisor's decisions publicly, without good reason, and makes that supervisor's position untenable.**

The remedy in such cases is to claim constructive dismissal through an industrial tribunal because the employer's behaviour showed that the company did not intend to be bound by the contract of employment. The procedure is the same as for unfair dismissal.

> If you would like to see an industrial tribunal in action, (there are about seventy all over the country), you can arrange a visit by contacting:
>
> Central Office of Tribunals
> Southgate Street
> Bury St Edmunds
> Suffolk IP33 2QA
>
> Telephone: 01284 762300

Responsibilities of Employers and Employees

A business exists to fulfil a purpose and achieve its business objectives. However, there are many areas of business activity where the law steps in and places constraints on what a business can and cannot do. Those areas include:

- **employees – the human resource;**
- **safety;**
- **environment;**
- **sale of goods and services;**
- **tax;**
- **insurance;**
- **stocks and shares;**
- **information.**

In order to be successful, managers must find ways of achieving their objectives within the law, without adding to their costs to such an extent that the business becomes uncompetitive.

In relation to human resources, the law confers rights and places responsibilities on both employers and employees. We have already discussed rights. Now, we consider the responsibilities of employers and employees.

Employer responsibilities

One way that employers ensure that they meet their legal responsibilities for employees is to plan. A **business plan** usually covers a period of three to five years. Most business plans contain:

- **growth objectives, perhaps in terms of new products, new markets and market share;**
- **financial objectives in the form of budgets, cost controls and profit;**
- **people objectives, in terms of numbers of staff, and performance levels.**

By setting out their objectives, companies can develop appropriate procedures and actions to ensure that laws are obeyed and that they meet their responsibilities to their employees. For example, a company will calculate the number and type of personnel that are required to achieve the business plan. It will ensure that its human resource policies are designed both to meet its business objectives and to satisfy all legal requirements. These policies include:

- **a recruitment and selection policy** that does not discriminate against candidates on grounds of their race, colour, creed or ethnic origin, and that respects equal opportunities legislation;
- **a training and development policy** which ensures that the knowledge and skills needed to achieve the business objectives are available to all;

- **policies and procedures** exist for promotion and transfer of employees between departments;
- **a pay policy** which sets out clearly the scales of pay that apply to each job class, and any additions to basic pay, such as overtime and holiday pay, together with a declared policy of equal pay for work of equal value;
- **sick pay** arrangements and pension schemes;
- **a health and safety policy** which ensures that the necessary organisation and arrangements are in place;
- **discipline and grievance procedures** which are fair to both employees and the employer.

Where trade unions are recognised by the employer, arrangements should be in place for negotiations to take place relating to pay, conditions, grievances, discipline and other employee relations issues within the scope of their recognition.

Employee responsibilities

As with the employer, employees also have responsibilities. The main responsibilities are:

- **to attend work, to be punctual and to abide by company rules;**
- **to work efficiently and to produce goods (or services) to the quality required;**
- **to comply with rules relating to equality and discrimination;**
- **to work safely, to comply with safety rules, and not to endanger self or others;**
- **to be loyal to the employer and to preserve the employer's trade secrets.**

The article below illustrates the damage that can occur if employees do not take their responsibilities seriously.

ACTIVITY

Read the article about the lecturer receiving damages for being insulted. This is a case of employees not complying with the rules relating to equality and discrimination.

Please do not laugh at it. Instead, list all the people and institutions that were or will be adversely affected by it. It could run into a big number, so think widely. For example, consider the effects if a member of staff faces disciplinary action. If that person was sacked, it could affect his or her students' education; it could affect his or her family, etc.

£30,000 damages for Irish insult

The award of nearly £30,000 damages to a college lecturer called an 'Irish prat' by a colleague was criticised by a Tory councillor as 'stupidly high'.

Alan Bryans, 43, a special needs tutor at a Northumberland College of Arts and Technology, was said by an industrial tribunal to have been victim of 'particularly appalling' racial discrimination.

Besides the 'prat' remark, he was nicknamed 'Gerry Adams' by fellow staff wanting him to move his car. On another occasion a woman lecturer embarrassed him by asking him to serenade her with an Irish song.

Mr Bryans became so distressed that he lost two stone in weight. He is still receiving stress counselling.

Bill Purdoe, a Conservative councillor, described the amount of damages as 'stupidly high for what appears to have been a relatively minor incident. This is an enormous amount of money for a small college to pay – £29,000 could cover a lecturer's salary for a year.'

Mr Bryans' case was supported by the Commission for Racial Equality. His solicitor said: 'People may say this was only a bit of mickey-taking, but those people should beware – racist jokes can have expensive punchlines.'

Daily Telegraph, 23 September 1995

TRADE UNIONS AND STAFF ASSOCIATIONS

An independent trade union is defined as 'an organisation that consists mainly of work people whose principal purpose is the regulation of relations between those people and their employers'. A full definition is given in the **Trade Union and Labour Relations Act 1974**.

Since the **Employment Act 1980**, there is no obligation on employers to recognise trade unions. An employer is free to refuse to recognise a trade union even where that union has a significant number of members among the company's employees. An employer can also decide to derecognise, without negotiation, a union which has members among the company's employees.

Trade union membership has declined from 13.3 million in 1979 to under 10 million at the present time. As well as the decline in numbers, legislation has reduced trade union powers and passed the 'right to manage' back to managers. Whether this is a good thing depends on your political outlook. Despite these major changes, unions play an important role in representing their members in the employee relations field.

An employer may decide to recognise a union for certain matters. The boundaries are set out in an agreement which includes a union's right to represent its members in all or any of the following:

- **pay and conditions of work;**
- **the physical conditions in which its members have to work;**
- **the fairness of the recruitment, selection and promotion processes;**
- **the ways people are dismissed or suspended;**
- **the ways work is allocated to people or teams;**
- **the ways the discipline and grievance procedures are used;**
- **membership or non-membership of a trade union;**
- **facilities for trade union officials;**
- **procedures for conducting negotiations between employer and union.**

An individual employee is relatively powerless in a dispute with an employer. So people join unions to give them a little more security – collectively they can expect to have more influence in bargaining with an employer. In this way, they hope that the power balance between employer and employee is fairer. Unions can also exert pressure on behalf of their members at a political level.

ACTIVITY

1. **Working with a colleague, prepare an argument supporting one of the following positions:**
   - **for union representation for employees in settling a dispute with an employer;**
   - **against union representation for employees in settling a dispute with an employer.**
2. **When you have a sound argument, arrange to put it to a pair of colleagues who have prepared the opposite argument. It is important that you use reasoned argument and hear the other side out. Don't heckle or interrupt.**
3. **When you have completed the exercise, look again at your argument and see if you still hold the same view, or have you amended it?**

The main tool of the union is **collective bargaining**. This is a technique for controlling the basic power relationships which underlie the conflict of interest in the employee relations system. Employers have a powerful advantage when negotiating with individual employees. Trade unions try to counter this advantage by negotiating on behalf of groups of employees, by presenting collective demands.

Employees and trade unions try to establish mutually-accepted rules and procedures that provide a relatively stable framework in which to negotiate. In essence, negotiations are about distributing scarce resources –

money, status and power. Negotiators can choose collaboration or conflict. But, by whichever route, agreement has to be reached eventually. Failure to agree by collaboration can result in **industrial action**.

ITN union staff vote to strike

Journalists and technicians at ITN voted yesterday to hold a two-hour strike which could disrupt news bulletins.

Union officials warned that the strike would be the first of a series – possibly escalating into 24 hour walkouts – unless talks resumed.

ITN's management says its programmes, including News At Ten and Channel 4 News, will be screened as normal.

Members of the National Union of Journalists and the Broadcasting, Entertainment, Cinematograph and Theatre Union are protesting at ITN's decision to abandon collective pay bargaining, which they claim amounts to union derecognition.

Of 333 NUJ and Bectu members balloted, 183 voted for industrial action. ITN's work force is 674. John Fray, the NUJ's national broadcasting organiser, said: "This is an overwhelming vote of no confidence in management's intentions, which will have to be modified to avoid the risk of serious disruption."

ITN said only a small proportion of staff had voted to strike. "We are confident there will be no disruption of transmission of programmes," said a spokeswoman.

Stewart Purvis, its chief executive, is to meet staff today for a briefing. He insists that management should be allowed to pay performance-related salaries.

The historically high salaries of Bectu staff "pose a consistent problem in negotiations for new television news business contracts in a fiercely competitive market", he said.

Guardian, 24 January 1996

Industrial action

Industrial action occurs when an employer and a union are in dispute and have failed to reach an agreement. The union's members use their collective power to 'put pressure' on the employer by:

- **non-co-operation – refusing to undertake work outside job descriptions;**
- **working to rule – doing only those tasks described in the job's 'rule book';**
- **withdrawal of labour – strike action.**

This is intended to bring the employer closer to the union's demands. Sometimes it works and sometimes it does not. One thing is certain, if it damages the business, no one wins.

Ford factories back to normal

FORD'S DAGENHAM and Southampton factories returned to normal yesterday after Thursday's wildcat strikes, which cost £10 million in lost production.

Union leaders will meet on Wednesday to discuss their next move after rejecting a 9.25 per cent wage increase over two years.

Daily Telegraph, 18 November 1995

Role of staff associations

Some employers who do not wish to recognise a trade union will encourage and finance the founding of a staff association. Staff associations invariably have little power. They pursue issues of common interest such as the provision of social events and recreational facilities. They rarely have any influence over the rights of employees, and have no negotiating rights over wages or conditions of employment. As they have no 'independence', staff associations cannot be compared with independent trade unions. They are often just a management concession to employees who wish to be consulted and have some say in the running of the business.

SETTLING INDUSTRIAL DISPUTES

If employers, trade unions and/or individual employees cannot resolve conflict, there are three bodies set up to arbitrate and adjudicate on industrial disputes. Below, we look in turn at the work of the Advisory, Conciliation and Arbitration Service, industrial tribunals and employment appeals tribunals.

ADVISORY, CONCILIATION AND ARBITRATION SERVICE

The Advisory, Conciliation and Arbitration Service (ACAS) is an independent body set up in 1976 to improve employee relations by offering an impartial service to both parties in an industrial dispute. It provides:

- **advice** to employers, employees and unions in matters of employee relations;
- **help to both sides** in resolving industrial disputes; this help might be in the form of advice or conciliation – if neither is effective, ACAS arbitrates between the sides in dispute, but it will do so only if both the union and the employer agree to be bound by ACAS's decision;
- **a code of practice and guidance** for disciplinary and grievance procedures.

ACAS has survived so long because it has maintained its impartiality, and is seen to be even handed in its dealing with both sides in a dispute. In Northern Ireland, the **Labour Relations Agency** provides a similar service.

ACTIVITY

ACAS produces excellent booklets on a wide range of employee relations issues. Write to them and ask for a list of its publications. Some are free and some are not. The address is:

Advisory, Conciliation and Arbitration Service
27 Wilton Street
London SW1X 7AZ
Telephone: 0171 210 3000

INDUSTRIAL TRIBUNALS

Any breach of contract that cannot be settled by other means may end up in a special court called an industrial tribunal.

Industrial tribunals are full members of the UK legal system. They are unique in having people on them who are chosen because they understand the work environment in matters relating to employment law. Each tribunal has a chairperson who is a barrister or solicitor with at least seven year's experience, plus two lay people, one drawn from panel of employer members, the other drawn from a panel of employee members. In some cases, a tribunal may sit without the lay members.

Industrial tribunals are more accessible to ordinary people than other courts. A complaint to an industrial tribunal by an employee or former employee is written on a very simple form – an IT1 – and sent to the tribunal office. There is no need to engage a solicitor or be represented at any hearing, although there is nothing to stop a person doing so if he or she wishes; about 50 per cent of applicants are legally represented. There are no court fees, and only in very exceptional circumstances are costs awarded against a person who loses a case. So it is easy and cheap to take a case to an industrial tribunal.

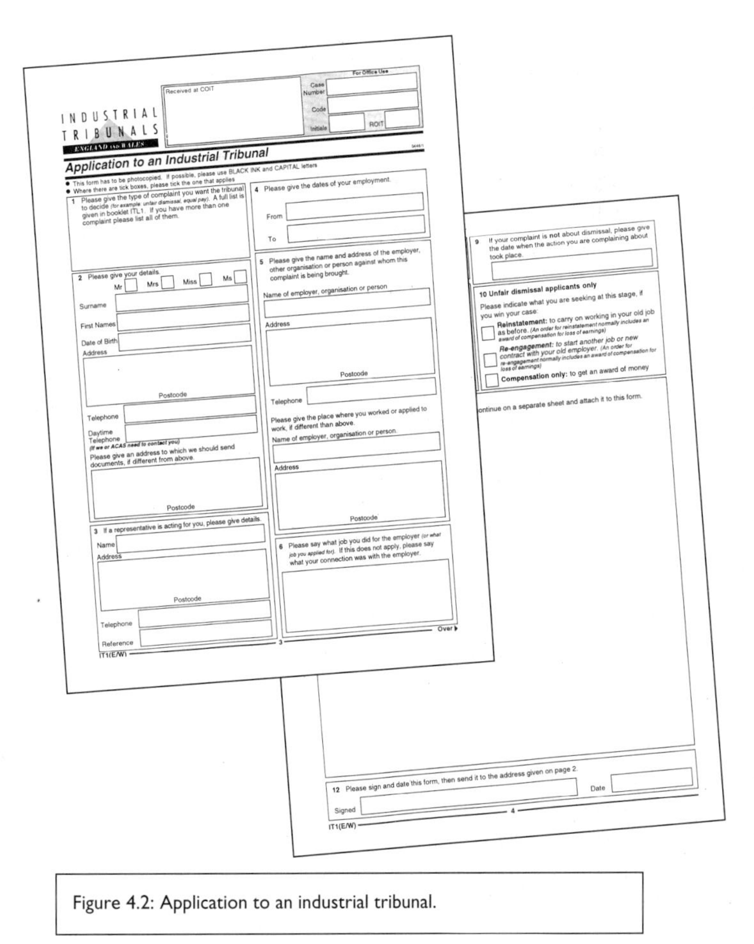

INDUSTRIAL TRIBUNALS
ENGLAND AND WALES

Received at COIT

For Office Use
Case Number
Code
Initials
ROIT

Application to an Industrial Tribunal

- This form has to be photocopied. If possible, please use BLACK INK and CAPITAL letters
- Where there are tick boxes, please tick the one that applies

1 Please give the type of complaint you want the tribunal to decide *(for example: unfair dismissal, equal pay)*. A full list is given in booklet ITL1. If you have more than one complaint please list all of them.

2 Please give your details.
Mr ☐ Mrs ☐ Miss ☐ Ms ☐
Surname
First Names
Date of Birth
Address
Postcode
Telephone
Daytime Telephone *(If we or ACAS need to contact you)*
Please give an address to which we should send documents, if different from above.
Postcode

3 If a representative is acting for you, please give details.
Name
Address
Postcode
Telephone
Reference

4 Please give the dates of your employment.
From
To

5 Please give the name and address of the employer, other organisation or person against whom this complaint is being brought.
Name of employer, organisation or person
Address
Postcode
Telephone
Please give the place where you worked or applied to work, if different than above.
Name of employer, organisation or person.
Address
Postcode

6 Please say what job you did for the employer *(or what job you applied for)*. If this does not apply, please say what your connection was with the employer.

Over ▸

IT1(E/W) 3

9 If your complaint is **not** about dismissal, please give the date when the action you are complaining about took place.

10 Unfair dismissal applicants only
Please indicate what you are seeking at this stage, if you win your case:
☐ **Reinstatement:** to carry on working in your old job as before. *(An order for reinstatement normally includes an award of compensation for loss of earnings)*
☐ **Re-engagement:** to start another job or new contract with your old employer. *(An order for re-engagement normally includes an award of compensation for loss of earnings)*
☐ **Compensation only:** to get an award of money

...ontinue on a separate sheet and attach it to this form.

12 Please sign and date this form, then send it to the address given on page 2.
Signed
Date

IT1(E/W) 4

Figure 4.2: Application to an industrial tribunal.

Industrial tribunals are probably best known for their powers to hear complaints of unfair dismissal. It is easy for an ex-employee to bring a complaint against the former employer. But to avoid wasting the tribunal's time, every complaint is vetted by ACAS which conciliates between the parties and tries to reach a settlement without the need to go before the tribunal.

In 1994, 46,000 complaints of unfair dismissal were lodged. The number of complaints has more than doubled since 1989. ACAS was able to settle over 19,000 out of tribunal. More than 11,000 complaints were dropped, and only 13,200 went on to be heard at tribunal.

Altogether, only about 44 per cent of complaints for unfair dismissal are upheld by tribunals. However, it is no victory for employers to win. They should be asking themselves: 'what went wrong to cause a complaint to be made to a tribunal?' If the answer shows that their procedures are being operated by the managers in the intended fashion, and that the procedures themselves are sufficient to meet their business objectives and legal requirements, then the case may be put down to a difficult employee. But in most cases, there will be evidence of a need to reappraise the way the organisation handles these difficult matters.

The stress imposed on managers who have to justify their actions to a tribunal is considerable. It is a costly business, taking up management time that could be spent on more productive matters. The cost to the company in time and expense, is considerable.

If an industrial tribunal finds that the complainant was unfairly dismissed, the former employee has a right to compensation, reinstatement or re-engagement.

Compensation is made up of several parts. There is a basic award of over £6,000. The tribunal can award additional compensation for loss of earnings, pension and so on, of £11,000. In addition, if the employer refuses to reinstate or re-engage, the former employee may be awarded further compensation. There is also a special award payable to those dismissed because of membership or non-membership of a trade union.

As well as facing the cost of meeting these substantial compensation awards, companies that dismiss employees unfairly also often receive considerable bad publicity in the press. The effect of bad publicity is impossible to measure.

EMPLOYMENT APPEAL TRIBUNAL

An appeal may be made on a point of law against a decision by a tribunal to an employment appeal tribunal. In 1994, 940 appeals were registered with the appeal tribunal. The majority were lodged by employees. The appeal tribunal is made up of a High Court judge and two lay people. They can uphold or overrule the findings of the industrial tribunal. In rare cases, appeals to the Court of Appeal, and then to the House of Lords can be allowed.

Judges dash hopes of backdated dismissal claims

Thousands of part-time workers attempting to bring compensation claims for unfair dismissal or redundancy that occurred more than two years ago had their hopes dashed by the Court of Appeal yesterday.

Three judges ruled that a House of Lords judgement in March 1994 giving part-timers working less than 16 hours a week the right to claim compensation did not apply retrospectively.

This means that part-timers who became eligible to bring claims after the Lords' judgement will succeed only if their claims were lodged within three months of their dismissal.

The ruling was given in a case brought by Mary Biggs, 56, who alleged she was unfairly dismissed in August 1976 after working for 17 months as a part-time science teacher in Shepton Mallet, Somerset.

At the time, she was unable to bring an unfair dismissal claim because she was working for only 14 hours a week and the qualifying period was then 21 hours. The Lords ruled that the then 16-hour qualifying period was in breach of European law because it discriminated against women. Within three months Mrs Biggs lodged an industrial tribunal claim in Exeter.

But the tribunal's decision that her claim was out of time and should have been lodged within three months of her dismissal in 1976 was upheld by the Employment Appeal Tribunal.

In the Court of Appeal, it was argued that it had not been practicable for Mrs Biggs to have brought her claim within three months of dismissal and the tribunal was bound by Community law to disregard the limits.

It was also argued that she could rely on directly-enforceable rights under Article 119 of the Treaty of Rome on which the Lords' judgement was based. But, in dismissing her appeal, the court ruled that it would have been possible for her to have made her claim within the time limit.

Daily Telegraph, 27 January 1996

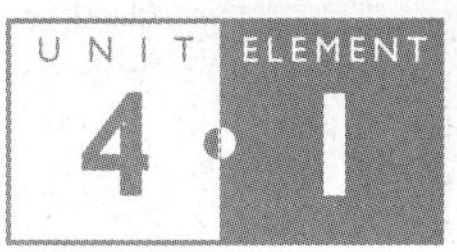

METHODS OF GAINING EMPLOYEE CO-OPERATION

Managing people is the most complex activity that a manager has to master. Some never master it. People are complex beings with both physical and mental needs. Although people's general characteristics can be categorised, each person is unique and is constantly changing and developing.

Physical needs include wages, sick pay, pensions, good conditions of work, safety, trade union recognition, contract of employment and business success.

Mental needs include good working relationships, a sense of belonging, knowing what is going on, self-esteem, respect, recognition for achievements, opportunity for personal improvement, a say in things that affect them, responsibility and autonomy.

To gain an employee's co-operation, all their needs should be satisfied to some extent at work. Many techniques have been developed to assist managers; each has some degree of success but they are only as good as the manager applying them. The case studies on page 20 illustrate some of the approaches that can be adopted.

ACTIVITY

Refer back to the list of items that must appear on the statement of terms and conditions of employment on page 5. Take each item from the list (do not bother about the first two – names and dates) and see where it fits into the 'model of human needs' illustrated in *Fig. 4.3*. For example, 'job title' fits into 'status'. Complete the picture of the relationship between the contract and the model of human needs.

Do you find that the contract meets mainly physical, rather than mental needs? If that is the case, we need to find other ways of satisfying mental needs at work.

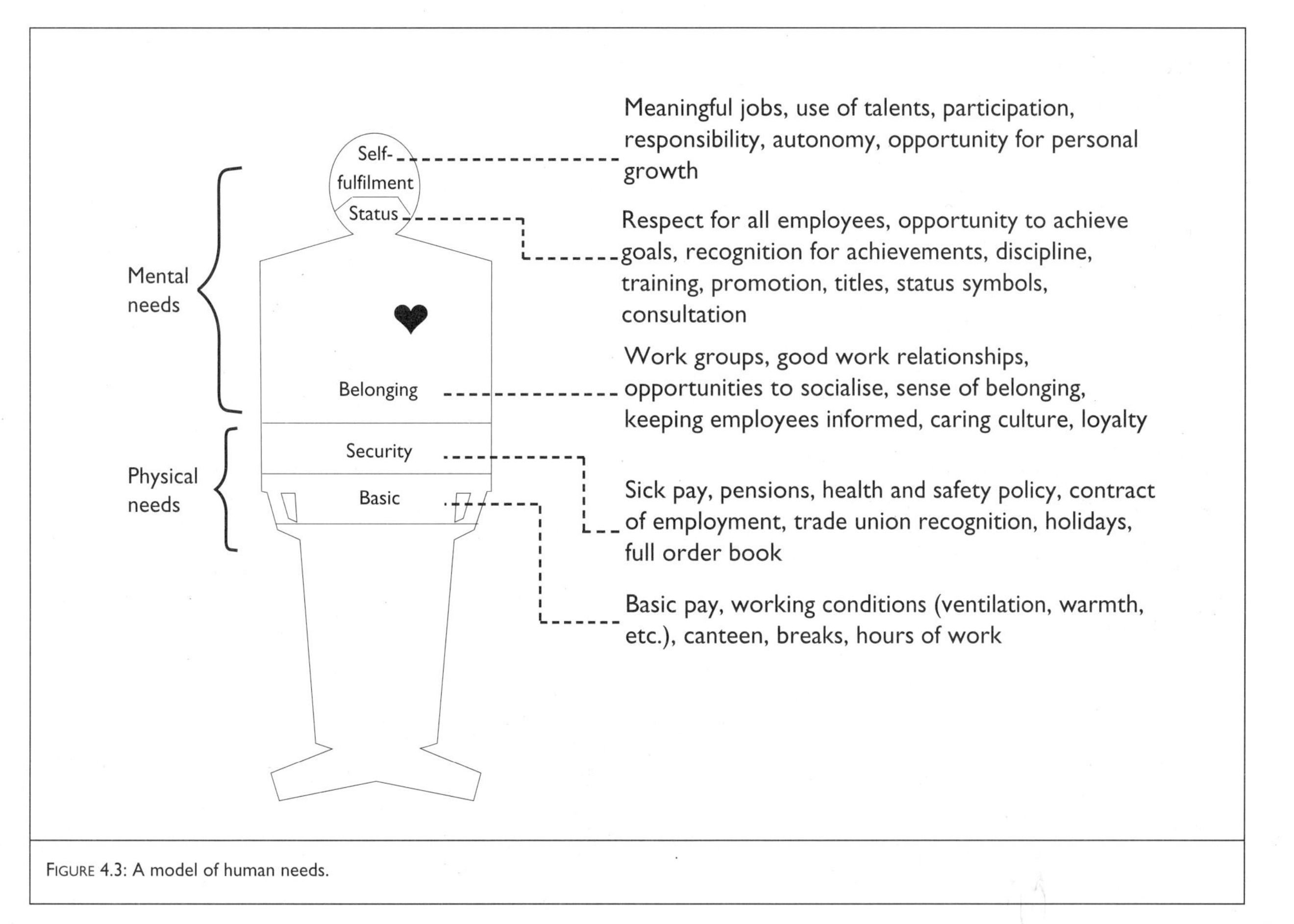

FIGURE 4.3: A model of human needs.

Bally Shoe Factories

In 1990, Bally Shoe Factories in Norwich was losing £1.5m on a turnover of £9m. Something had to be done. The company's operations director believed that there had to be revolutionary change. But what?

He visited twelve UK companies, including Nissan, and began to realise that Bally's own operations were out of balance. Seeing the success of other companies gave him and his colleagues courage to make some revolutionary changes.

There were two main thrusts. First, they decided to change Bally's market position to high price, high quality. Second, they sought to build much more trust and commitment with the employees.

To achieve the latter objective, they abandoned some traditional practices. They removed piecework, removed clock cards, stopped providing company cars to senior staff, and removed barriers between the managers and their staff. They developed effective ways of involving their employees in decision taking, making them aware of the value they added to the organisation.

All the changes – and the advice they sought from other companies – has been worth it. 'We were looking to break into profit in 1995,' said the operations director, 'but we actually achieved it in 1994.'

Bally's successful revolution has been based on rethinking its whole approach to its business. It moved from producing lower-priced shoes, and refocused its marketing effort to the higher end of the market. But the most impressive change has been to revise its culture from 'employees are different from managers' to 'employees are the same as managers'. The **single-status environment**!

It is often the case that people doing a job know more about its detail than the manager responsible for direct supervision. It is good sense, therefore, to develop groups (like quality circles) through which employees can give their expert advice and views to their manager. Consultation makes people feel valued, particularly when they can see that their advice is used to improve performance.

Design to Distribution

Design to Distribution, (D2D) supplies high-volume, printed circuit boards and products for a range of blue chip companies, including Dell, Hewlett Packard and Pace Micro Technology.

D2D is an example of world-class manufacturing leadership. It has achieved this enviable status by ensuring a pursuit of excellence and continuous improvement in every part of its business. To achieve this, every employee is considered a business driver. 'An operator working on a line knows the customer, the volume target, the board costs, the profit margins and, therefore, the number that we need to make in order to break even,' said D2D's quality and business planning manager.

In order to become world class other changes have been made. Operators now make decisions and deal with deviations in quality before they become problems; supervisors are more actively involved; and people from the plant have close contact with the customers. Operators are involved in the quality process rather than quality analysts – it's the only way to handle things quickly, as the customer wants. Operators are trained to carry out statistical process control. 'We don't measure as many things as we used to, but we certainly measure them more intelligently' said D2D's general manager.

▸▸▸

> Training is not undertaken in isolation without the commitment of every employee. Days are spent explaining the importance of the quality ethos; operators get to meet the customers and publicly sign their commitment to the goal of zero defects.
>
> These are all part of ongoing improvements that are needed to keep D2D world class.

Once again, employees – the human resource – play a key part in the company's strategy. As well as the investment in advanced technology, Design to Distribution treats all staff as vital partners in creating success. It creates teams that include customers, and gives operators control over their own work area. Training, and developing good attitudes, is seen to be at the heart of the move towards world-class status.

There is an emphasis on **team working**. Most people need to work with others to achieve their job objectives. You might know the positive feeling that comes from being a member of a successful team. By creating work teams and giving them authority to use available resources, employers can make teams responsible for achieving targets, and reward them for success. Knowledge about creating balanced teams has increased over the last fifteen years. As a result, expert managers can use this knowledge to form very effective teams which prove to be more productive than keeping people working as individuals. Most people enjoy being a part of a successful team and achieving good results for which they get recognition.

Operators and shop-floor workers are given more responsibility for quality. **Quality circles** are based on the belief that several heads are better than one. Allowing people to pool their experience and expertise to examine problems and offer solutions is both good business sense and good motivation. A strategy of seeking **continuous improvement** has proved to be a great motivator and creates a feeling of worth.

A common theme in these two case studies is the pursuit of success through people. One thing that results from being a contributor to success is a feeling of personal worth. There is a virtuous circle: the more people feel valued, the greater their self-esteem, then the greater their contribution. Together, these case studies give an idea of the methods that are being employed in the best British companies to gain employee co-operation and, through that, success.

Not every company meets these high standards and ideals. In 1996, many employees in the UK are suffering from a 'lack of security', even though the UK is supposed to be pulling out of the recession of the early 1990s faster than any other country in Europe. Feeling secure in your job generates the so-called 'feel-good factor'. It is good sense for successful employers to give as much assurance as possible about job security. Insecurity causes low morale; if company morale is low, the effectiveness of schemes to gain employee co-operation will be lessened.

The best way to secure co-operation is to:

- **treat people as adults;**
- **show them respect and value their expertise;**
- **involve them and consult them about plans;**
- **be open and honest and communicate clearly;**
- **give people lots of positive feedback on their performance;**
- **never forget to recognise good performance;**
- **always examine poor performance and find ways of preventing it happening again;**
- **let people learn – encourage personal development.**

PORTFOLIO ASSIGNMENT

This assignment is an investigation into the human resource and personnel policies of organisations. You are to research the policies of two organisations and to prepare a business report.

This assignment requires you to do a considerable amount of research. The research should provide the information you will need to write the report. Try to avoid the temptation to leave this piece of work until the last moment – you must allow time for busy business people to answer your requests for information and for their replies to arrive.

Your report should describe the human resource and personnel policies of two organisations. It should focus on:

- their health and safety policies and how these policies are carried out by managers and staff;
- their equal opportunities policies and how they are carried out and monitored by each company's managers;
- the actions that can be taken in each of your two organisations by employees if employers do not carry out their health and safety and equal opportunities obligations;
- the actions that can be taken by the employer if an employee does not co-operate with the organisation's health and safety and equal opportunities policies;
- the role that trade unions and staff associations play in negotiating pay and conditions of work and in providing information, advice and legal representation for their members.

In addition, for one of the two organisations, you should also report on how it:

- negotiates pay and conditions;
- handles disciplinary procedures;
- handles grievances;
- gains the co-operation of its employees.

Before beginning the research, ask your teacher if you are to work alone or if you can work in small groups to collect and share the data needed. If you work in small groups, you must write the report yourself, and show clearly your individual contribution to the research.

TASK 1

The first task is to prepare a research brief. You need to work out how to gather the data you need to write your report. Think of the different ways you can gather data to enable you to write an accurate report for this assignment.

Because of the complexity of this assignment, it might be best to design a questionnaire that covers all the topics specified in the assignment. In writing questions ask yourself whether they will produce the answers that give the information needed to write an informative, practical report.

You are going to have to get information from busy, professional people. So, it is important that your questionnaire is as clear and as short as possible. You should test out the questionnaire. Get a friend or colleague to read through it to see if they understand the questions. Let your teacher see the questionnaire and comment on it before you start your research.

Task 2

Your next task is to select two organisations for your research. Choose any two organisations you like. Here are a few suggestions:

- your school or college;
- a manufacturing business;
- a hospital;
- a commercial business, say a bank or building society;
- a branch of a trade union;
- a department store;
- a farming or agricultural business;
- a mine or quarry;
- a sports centre;
- a government department, say the education department of the metropolitan or county council.

Ideally, you want to approach organisations that are local. The best source might be organisations you know through your part-time work, through work experience placements, through friends or relatives, through your school or college work experience co-ordinator, or through your own initiative.

If these are not acceptable to you, you can find a lot more ideas in the Yellow Pages, Thompson's Directory, or the Chamber of Commerce Directory. Librarians will be able to show you what directories are available.

Task 3

To conduct the research, you need to approach the organisations that you have chosen. You need to find out which person can best answer your questions. In many cases, the best source of information is likely to be the organisation's human resources or personnel manager.

So you might write to the human resources manager. You could design your own letter-headed paper using a computer which depicts the fact that you are a GNVQ student at your school or college. Make it look professional and mature. Your letter is to explain that you need some information about human resourcing to help you complete this assignment; you might enclose a copy of the assignment if you think it would help to gain the manager's co-operation. Enclose a copy of your questionnaire.

If you do not wish to write, you may plan a telephone call that will serve the same purpose as the letter. You will need to follow this up by sending your questionnaire or arranging an interview with the appropriate managers.

Task 4

When you have received responses to your questionnaire and any other information that you need, you need to make sense of it. You need to think about the structure of your report. Note down the headings you intend to use, and transfer all the key information under the relevant headings.

Review the information you have gathered against what you have learnt about the contract of employment. Consider whether the organisations meet the requirements of

the law. Are the rights and duties of each party to the contract respected? In preparing and writing your report, you should include a summary of the main legal obligations under each of your headings.

TASK 5

The report is designed to show that you understand how human resource policies operate in local organisations and how these relate to the legal obligations imposed on employers and employees.

The report should have a structure that makes it easy for readers to understand and follow your findings. It should adopt the conventions and formats used in business reports. Agree a suitable format with your teacher before you write the final report.

Make sure that it is well presented. It should be word processed and spell checked. If appropriate, use tables and charts in the text to support your explanations.

Investigate job roles and changing working conditions

The structure of business organisations and their ownership is examined in unit 2. In this element, we examine some of the key management roles in business organisations, concentrating on the responsibility which managers have for employees – the human resource. We also consider the reasons why there have to be changes in the ways businesses are run.

Economists describe three resources of business – land, labour and capital. The business manager would break these down further.

- **Land – buildings; plant; machinery; materials; transport.**
- **People – knowledge; expertise; skills; experience; time; and energy.**
- **Capital – fixed capital; working capital; cash flow.**

Every business organisation, whether it is a charity, a school or a profit-making enterprise, needs resources to achieve its goals. The process of manipulating these resources effectively is called **'managing'**.

THE JOB OF MANAGING

There are many definitions of managing. The *Collins Dictionary* definition is 'having administrative control or authority'. Consider, now, the features of the manager's role.

- **Managers are responsible for achieving objectives.**
- **Managers work within a structured organisation and with prescribed roles.**
- **Managers use the formal authority that goes with their role to oversee the activities and performance of their staff.**
- **Managers use administrative systems and procedures to help meet stated objectives.**
- **Each manager is accountable to a more senior manager for the outcomes of the work undertaken under their authority.**

So, we could come up with a fuller definition and say that a manager has **authority** to manipulate the organisation's resources to achieve its objectives. The manager is **responsible** for using the resources only for the purpose intended, and is **accountable** to the owners of the resources for the achievement of the objectives.

ACTIVITIES OF MANAGERS

There are six main activities that managers carry out:

- **planning;**
- **organising;**
- **motivating;**
- **reviewing;**
- **communicating;**
- **co-ordinating.**

PLANNING

A plan is a design for achieving something. Planning takes place at all levels within an organisation. Plans can relate to short or long-term intentions.

Short-term plans are often called **tactical plans** and usually contain precise, detailed, measurable objectives. Short-term planning is carried out at lower levels in an organisation, at middle manager and supervisor levels.

Long-term plans are often called **strategic plans**. Long-term plans are not as detailed or measurable as short-term plans – the further you look into the future, the less certain managers can be about outcomes. They are usually made at higher levels of management.

ORGANISING

A plan on its own is a sterile thing. Nothing happens until it is turned into actions. A manager takes the resources (including people) which are allocated to a job and deploys them in such a way as to achieve the objectives.

MOTIVATING

Motivating refers to any activity carried out by a manager to obtain the co-operation of everyone who can affect the outcome of a job. Getting the optimum return from each person is in the interest of the whole organisation. Just think of the people who can affect outcomes: customers, suppliers, the manager's own staff, the boss, people in other departments, and so on. All of these must be 'motivated' to co-operate by the manager.

REVIEWING

Having made a plan and put it into action, a manager constantly reviews progress to ensure that the plan is working properly – that is, if the current activities are continued, the desired outcome will be achieved. If not, the manager modifies the activities to correct the situation. Usually there are management information systems (MIS) and procedures to ensure that relevant feedback about progress is available to the manager at all times.

COMMUNICATING

In all aspects of managing, and in all functions in an organisation, the degree of success is directly related to the quality of communication. It is the 'nervous system' of managing. (A more detailed treatment of this topic is contained in unit 2.) Managers should ensure that everyone knows and understands the importance of their contribution to business success. Staff should receive regular feedback from their managers about how they are performing against standards.

CO-ORDINATING

Managers deploy the available resources to the different tasks that need to be done to achieve objectives. Provided that all the tasks are completed successfully (that is, each

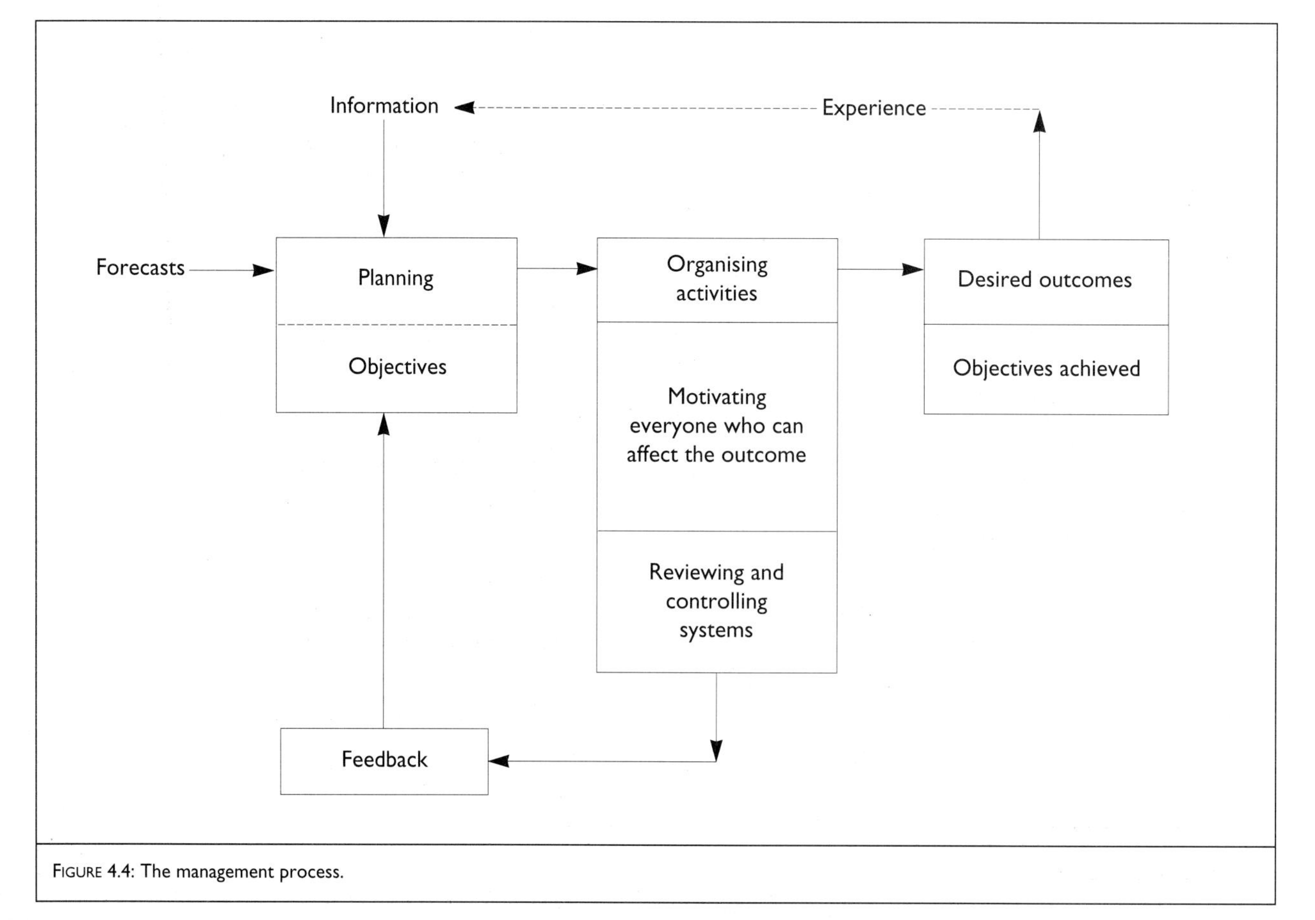

FIGURE 4.4: The management process.

meet its targets for quality, quantity, time and costs), their combined results will achieve the overall objective. Management information systems and operating procedures are designed to give the information to ensure that everyone is pulling in the same direction. Co-ordination is a unifying and harmonising activity.

Managing takes place at different levels in an organisation. The higher the level, the more general and strategic the work. The lower the level, the more tactical and specific the work. Although six levels are shown in *Fig. 4.5*, many of these levels are combined in medium and small enterprises. However, these smaller organisations still distinguish between strategic and tactical objectives.

ACTIVITY

We all 'manage' things. For example, we manage a lot of our social activities.

Imagine you are going on holiday with three friends and it has fallen to you to make all the arrangements. Using each of the six main activities of managing, prepare a report for your three friends of all the activities that have to be carried out (under each activity) to ensure you have a great holiday.

For example, the first thing you might do is plan a meeting where you will all decide where to go. List the resources you would need for that meeting.

For this exercise, assume that money is not a problem (if only!) – you can have whatever it costs.

Level	Role
Owners or shareholders	Provide the resources for the enterprise
Board of directors	Entrusted with the resources. Makes policy and gives direction to the organisation. Determines strategic objectives
Senior managers	Clarify objectives; plan work; organise and distribute activities; allocate resources
Managers	Determine tactical objectives; distribute tasks to other people; direct activities of subordinate staff
Supervisors	Allocate tasks and materials to individuals; monitor and control performance of others
Operatives	Employ their expertise and experience to produce the planned output required to achieve objectives

FIGURE 4.5: Levels of authority.

DELEGATION

In order to get all the work done within an organisation, it is necessary to pass authority to lower levels of management. *Fig. 4.6* shows how authority is passed down an organisation.

By delegating authority, managers at lower levels within an organisation get the right to use the organisation's resources to produce products or services. Without authority, no manager at any level has the right to use resources – it could be fraud or theft to do so. If authority is delegated to a supervisor by his or her boss, the supervisor can use staff time by giving them work to do, spend money within budget, use raw materials, and so on.

The supervisor is now responsible for ensuring that the staff work efficiently on the job, use the materials for the products or services intended, and spend the budget only on things relating to the job. As the job proceeds, the supervisor has to account to his or her boss for the resources used, by showing the output created by their use. If targets are being met, all is well. If targets are not being met, the supervisor will be expected to take corrective action to get back on target.

You cannot get rid of accountability by delegating authority. The supervisor's boss has to answer to his or her boss in the same way. So you can see that it is not valid management behaviour to 'blame' subordinates for poor performance. They, the higher-level managers, are accountable for the performance of all their resources.

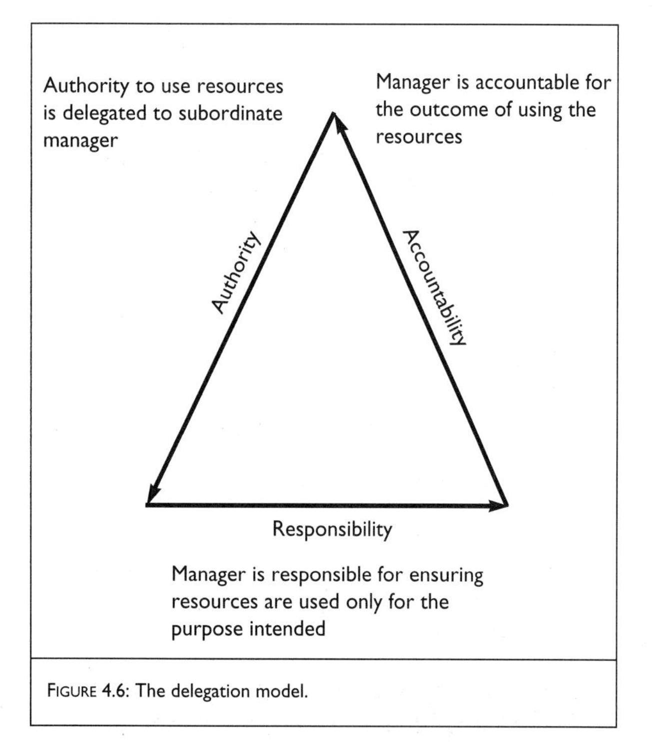

FIGURE 4.6: The delegation model.

ACTIVITY

Read the section on delegation carefully, focusing on all the people involved, upwards, downwards, and sideways. Write a short essay which examines the place of 'trust' in the delegation process.

DIRECTORS

Directors are the most senior managers in a public or private limited company. In other types of organisation, such as a county council, there will be similar roles but possibly bearing different titles, like chief executive, for example.

Directors are nominated by the board of directors and appointed by the shareholders. The shareholders delegate authority to the board to manage their resources for the success of the business on a day-to-day basis. The directors are **responsible** for seeing that the resources are used only for the purpose intended and they are **accountable** to the shareholders for the outcomes of their management. If the shareholders are not satisfied with the performance of the directors, they may try to remove them from managing the company's affairs. This is a complex process and is seldom attempted.

Directors have their duties described in legal documents called the **memorandum and articles of association**. They may take any actions needed to run the business on a day-to-day basis, provided they are not unlawful under the Companies Acts 1985. Directors have duties in common law. You will recall from our discussion about the contract of employment that duties of care and skill arise in common law. Directors must not act negligently in managing the company's affairs.

Before looking at the duties of directors in a little more detail, it is worth quoting again from case law. In the case *Re v City Equitable Fire Insurance Co (1925)*, the judge commented: 'It is indeed impossible to describe the duties of directors in general terms ... The position of a director of a company carrying on a small retail business is very different from that of a director of a railway company.'

ROLES OF DIRECTORS

The **managing director** is the most senior director on the board. Although there is no legal requirement to have a managing director, it is unusual to find a board without one.

If a managing director is appointed by a decision of the board, he or she acts in two capacities. First, as a director, all the powers, rights and duties associated with directorships apply to the managing director. Second, the board can delegate to the managing director the authority to make decisions that would normally be made by the whole board.

A **chairperson to the board** can also be appointed to preside at every board meeting and facilitate good practice. Often the chairperson is non-executive, that is, he or she does not work within the company and simply brings special expertise to the board meetings.

Non-executive directors do not work full-time in the business. As with non-executive chairpersons, the non-executive directors bring special skills or experience to the board to enhance the decisions taken. A non-executive director can be charged with negligence in the same way as an ordinary director.

The attributes of directors

Directors need knowledge, skills and experience at two levels.

First, they should have functional expertise. For example, one director might be an engineer with responsibility for advising the board on production matters. Similarly, one would advise on financial matters, another on marketing matters, and another on human resource matters.

Second, each director should be a skilled manager. They should each be capable of:

- **planning at a strategic level;**
- **obtaining and organising resources;**
- **using social and human skills to maintain morale;**
- **offering leadership;**
- **communicating clearly;**
- **gathering and interpreting information;**
- **solving problems;**
- **taking high-level decisions.**

Directors should also be able to visualise what the business should look like in five or ten years time and start building for that now.

ACTIVITY

For this activity you will need access to a broadsheet newspaper, such as *The Times* or the *Daily Telegraph*. Turn to the business section. Many articles refer to the activities of directors and senior managers. For example, the front page of the *Sunday Times* business section on 3 December 1995 contained six stories, five of which had quotations from named senior managers.

1. **Try to work out from these articles the sorts of activities that directors and senior managers undertake.**
2. **Make a list of all the activities you can identify and describe the skills needed to carry them out.**

Directors' responsibilities for human resources

The board of directors is responsible for formulating a human resource policy. This policy would be passed down to managers who would ensure that it is followed by everyone in the organisation.

In practice, a human resources policy might be divided into a number of policies covering different aspects of personnel management. These might include:

- **equal opportunities policy;**
- **equal pay policy;**
- **non-discrimination policy;**
- **health, safety and welfare policy;**
- **pension arrangements;**
- **sick pay policy;**
- **management policies for morale and motivation;**
- **management policies relating to changes needed for future success.**

Although directors do not usually get involved in the day-to-day implementation of these policies, it is good practice for reports about their effectiveness to be presented to the board by the accountable manager on a regular basis – say, twice or four times a year.

MANAGERS

There is usually a manager in charge of each function in an organisation. Like directors, they need to be experienced and skilled in both their specialist function and in the skills of managing a department and its people.

Managers take the policies passed down from the board and turn them into activities. These activities are designed to achieve the corporate goals; a manager has no authority to use resources for any other purpose.

For example, the human resources director will hand down the human resources policy to the human resources managers. They will design procedures and processes to ensure that the policy is implemented throughout the organisation and that its goals are achieved. The human resources managers will need to consult with operational managers, and then plan and organise procedures for:

- **planning the numbers and types of staff** the organisation needs in the future;
- **attracting sufficient candidates** with the right qualities so that the organisation can select the best people for jobs;
- **training and developing staff** so that they perform to the highest level possible;
- **designing jobs** that are stimulating and interesting so that the organisation gets the best out of people;
- **ensuring that organisational structures and procedures** allow employees to have their views, ideas, worries and disputes heard;
- **designing ways of introducing and managing change** that minimise any negative impact on individuals and groups;
- **providing fair and legal procedures** for discipline and grievances, and ensuring they are applied uniformly throughout the organisation;
- **keeping within the law** on issues such as health and safety, equal opportunities, sex and race discrimination, and termination of employment;
- **dealing with trade unions,** staff associations, disputes, industrial tribunals and other legal actions.

ACTIVITY

Consider these questions about training policy. Write a short report (two pages) with your views, supported by reasoned argument.

1 Who should be responsible for identifying the training needs of operatives in:

(a) a manufacturing business;
(b) an insurance company?

2 Who should carry out the training?

3 Who should record the training (and qualifications) held by employees?

4 Who should authorise the finance for the training?

A human resources manager has objectives relating to:

- **the size and make-up of the organisation's workforce;**
- **salary negotiations and salary budget;**
- **training plans and training budget;**
- **staff turnover and morale;**
- **handling of disputes with individuals and unions.**

ACTIVITY

If you have a human resources manager (sometimes called a personnel manager) in your school or college, ask your tutor to invite him or her to give you a talk about human resources objectives.

SUPERVISORS

Supervisors are usually the first level of management in an organisation. They tend to be very skilled in the work of their department and are often promoted from within the department. They have daily face-to-face contact with their staff and deal with matters that require immediate attention. Sometimes supervisors are considered as the 'meat in the sandwich' because they are not considered a part of management, nor are they considered a part of the operational staff.

However, supervisors have management responsibilities. Departmental supervisors would be expected to manage their staff so that the department's objectives are achieved. They must operate within the contract of employment, within the law and within any procedures set out by the human resources manager. They are expected to manage staff effectively, to ensure their competence, and to ensure that high morale is maintained. Supervisors are perhaps best placed to decide upon performance standards for their staff, to monitor their actual work, to either coach them to achieve better performance or to organise their training, and to deal with day-to-day issues that might arise, such as discipline or grievance.

If a supervisor has insufficient knowledge about specialist human resource issues, he or she can call upon the human resources manager. In general, the human resources manager's role would be to advise supervisors on the handling of specialist matters only – those that might have a legal implication or such like.

ACTIVITY

Read the article opposite. Now consider a situation where a business decides to disband its human resources department and devolve 'power' to departmental managers. The department had been running for ten years with five personnel specialists.

You are one of these departmental managers. Prepare a short presentation to the managing director explaining all the steps that would have to be taken to ensure that this change could be implemented with minimum disruption.

Personnel officers are a waste of time, says new study

A team of academics led by Professor David Metcalf at the London School of Economics (LSE) has analysed job performance in 2,000 workplaces. They found that personnel directors on the board or specialist personnel officers in the workplace detracted from a company's performance.

The climate of management-employee relations was worse, productivity poorer and staff turnover rates higher when personnel managers were in place. Although human resource techniques – employee involvement, merit pay rises and blurring distinctions between managers and workers – did work, their success had nothing to do with the presence of personnel officers.

The LSE researchers' biggest problem is to explain why the work of personnel officers is not merely irrelevant but positively malign. Sue Fernie, one of the academic team, said: 'Workers see a personnel department as an external agency which distances them from their company and knows little about their work.'

Many companies are coming to the same conclusion. Only 30 per cent of British companies had a personnel officer on the board in 1993 against 70 per cent in the early 1980s. Tesco, British Gas and the RAC are all joining the list of large companies cutting or reorganising personnel departments.

It was in the 1960s that personnel work became a growth industry. Now industry has coined new buzzwords such as 'delayering' and 'flattening out the pyramid'. In practice, it means firms are devolving power to departmental managers from remote personnel officials.

But paradoxically, just as businesses are giving fewer jobs to specialist personnel officers, the government is stuffing them into quangos in the cause of making the public sector more business-like.

'NHS Trusts and further education colleges are all getting them,' said Ms Fernie. 'The anecdotal evidence we are getting is that they are helping to make relations between management and staff absolutely dire.'

Independent on Sunday, 15 May 1994

Managing change

Nobody can be unaware of the enormous changes that are taking place in businesses throughout the world. There is a range of forces that are acting on businesses which make change inevitable. If businesses do not respond positively and imaginatively to these forces they will almost certainly cease to exist in their present form. The greatest forces on businesses to change are:

- **new technology;**
- **world markets;**
- **changing work patterns;**
- **workforce demands;**
- **environmental pressure groups.**

New technology

The rate of technological change is accelerating. It permeates every aspect of business activity: design, production planning, production control, automated production, warehousing, despatch, transportation, administration systems, management information systems, and so on. Robotics, automation and information technology are in their early stages of development. As progress continues the nature of industry and commerce will change even more dramatically. This topic is covered more fully in unit 2.

World markets

International companies are able to exploit world markets, enjoying considerable economies of scale as transport and communication unit costs decline. World-wide production facilities, automation, and 'instant information' anywhere in the world, have changed the nature of competition. Companies which do not deliver quality goods on time are being bypassed. Consumers demand more choice and new products. Product life cycles are shortening and product development timescales have had to speed up. Technological 'designer' products are replacing traditional versions. Premium brands are being overtaken by supermarkets' own brands – the power has shifted from the 'ability to advertise heavily' to the organisations that own the shelf space.

Changing work patterns

The changes in technology and world markets are beginning to have an impact on the composition of the workforce. So, too, has the growth of service industries and the decline of manufacturing industries. There is less demand for unskilled and semi-skilled people, and growing demand for technocrats. There are greater numbers of people going to university. There is an explosion of technical and scientific journals which carry up-to-date knowledge to businesses. There are more imaginative working patterns – part-time working, job sharing, 'hot desking', working from home, and so on.

Workforce demands

As employees become more expert and more aware, they are demanding better working conditions and a better quality of working life. They want to be consulted about matters that affect them at work. They have higher expectations about work than previous generations; people are not likely to become committed to employers who do not consider their needs and expectations. They want job satisfaction and know how to get it.

Environmental pressure groups

Businesses are concerned to maintain a good relationship with their suppliers and customers. Highly intelligent people in pressure groups now monitor the workings of businesses and bring to public notice any environmentally unfriendly practices they find. This can damage a company's reputation and give its competitors an advantage. There have been examples of pressure groups staging high-profile demonstrations against a particular company and organising boycotts of its products. This makes businesses consider their practices very carefully to avoid 'upsetting' these groups.

Why businesses must change

In response to these forces, businesses are having to adapt to new ways and to adopt new methods. There are good business reasons why they accept the need to change. They may embrace change:

- **to improve efficiency and effectiveness;**
- **to improve profits;**
- **to respond to, or get ahead of competition;**
- **to adopt new technology;**
- **to comply with government or European Union regulations;**
- **to introduce new products or services;**
- **to take account of public pressure;**
- **to grow and become more influential.**

You can see that the benefits of implementing changes for the business are quite attractive – increased profitability, faster growth than competitors, 'better' products than competitors, good public relations and more power in the marketplace.

IMPLEMENTING CHANGE

In order to implement changes, management must first understand why most people fear or resist change. Only if they take these reasons into account, will they be able to implement changes as quickly and successfully as Japanese industry.

REASONS FOR RESISTANCE TO CHANGE

People resist change for very good reasons; it is a normal human response which competent managers understand and deal with professionally. Change generates all sorts of fears. People fear the unknown and they are likely to feel insecure if they do not understand how change will affect them. Employees – including many managers – fear that:

- **they might lose their job and hence their livelihood;**
- **they might not be able to handle new responsibilities;**
- **they might lose status, particularly if they are very good at their current job;**
- **they might have to change their work group and, perhaps, their social life, maybe even having to move home;**
- **they might be unable to do work they like, devaluing their skills;**
- **change is being introduced for change's sake – we have always done it this way, so why change?**
- **change will not work – it has been tried before and failed, so it will not work this time;**
- **their skills might become obsolete;**
- **they might have even more work and be under even greater pressure.**

So, businesses must change, and there is nothing wrong with that; and people resist or fear change, and that is a very normal human reaction. How can these conflicting positions be reconciled?

ACTIVITY

1 **Look at the two lists above, the reasons why businesses embrace change and the reasons why people fear and resist change. Classify each reason as either having to do with technology, the achievement of organisational goals, or outside influences (mark these reasons 'T'), or primarily concerned with social relationships, personal fears or motivations, or how hard an individual might have to work (mark these reasons 'S').**

2 **Now count the number of Ts and Ss you have put against each list. Calculate the percentage of reasons that you classified T and S respectively. Write your answers in a matrix like this:**

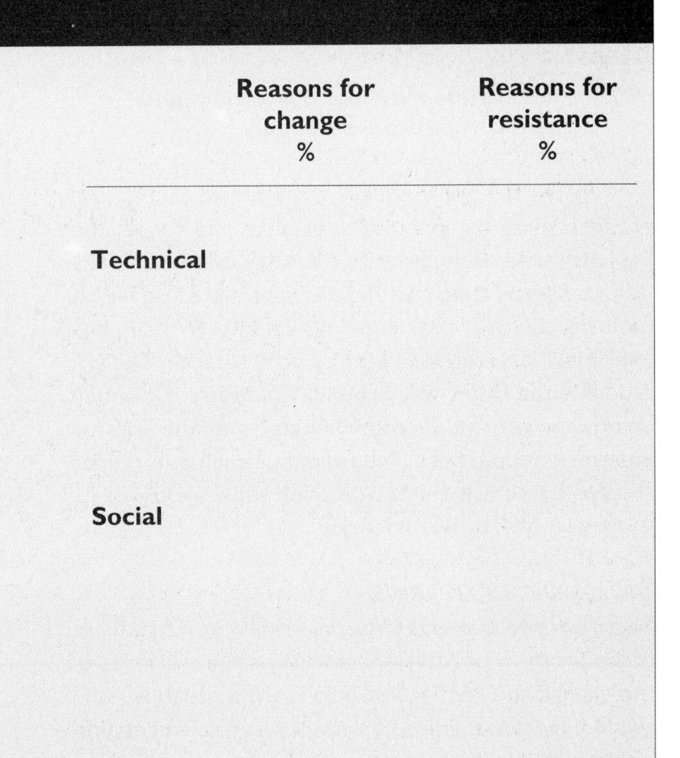

	Reasons for change %	Reasons for resistance %
Technical		
Social		

When business managers complete a similar activity, their results show on average that 80 per cent of the 'reasons for change' are T reasons and only 20 per cent are S reasons. Conversely, only 20 per cent of 'the reasons for resistance' are T reasons and 80 per cent are S reasons.

This analysis highlights a real difficulty. Reasons for change are likely to be communicated in technical terms, while people want to know answers to the social question: 'how does change affect me?' Until this 'great change question' is answered, the fears – and consequently the resistance – will not decline.

If a business needs to change to keep competitive, and that change is resisted by employees, and managers have not answered the 'great change question', it will have detrimental effects on the business. These include:

- **the changes are more costly to implement;**
- **the changes take longer to implement, wasting time;**
- **the business receives the benefits of the change later and loses potential income;**
- **the morale of the employees suffers, affecting performance;**
- **there may be industrial unrest, creating poor publicity;**
- **the business may lose customers and make competitors stronger.**

You can see that it is a key management skill to plan changes so as to minimise resistance and to get the implementation completed as smoothly as possible. The Japanese spend time planning a change and explaining it until people are clear and understand it; then they implement it quickly with little or no resistance. The UK model is the other way around. Changes are planned quickly and very little is communicated until the time for implementation comes. Then the implementation tends to take longer with much disruption while people resist and try to stick to the old ways.

Developing an approach

There are two elements to planning a change. First, there is the problem of really understanding the dynamics of the change and 'getting a handle' on the situation. And second, there is the need to develop an implementation plan which enables the change to be made quickly and with minimum resistance.

Force field analysis

If you imagine a blown-up balloon, it will stay that size so long as the pressure (force) inside is the same as the pressure (force) outside. If you alter either pressure, the balloon changes size. If the pressure inside is reduced compared with the pressure outside, it will change to a smaller size. If the pressure inside increases compared with the pressure outside, it will change to a larger size.

In this case, the change is brought about by changing one of the forces. This concept can be applied to any change to help us understand the dynamics of the situation.

In any stable situation, there are restraining forces pushing it one way and driving forces pushing it the other way. If both these forces are balanced, the situation will remain stable. If you want to change the situation, all you have to do is identify the nature of the restraining and driving forces, and then alter one or more of the forces to drive it in the direction you want. Just like letting some air out of the balloon.

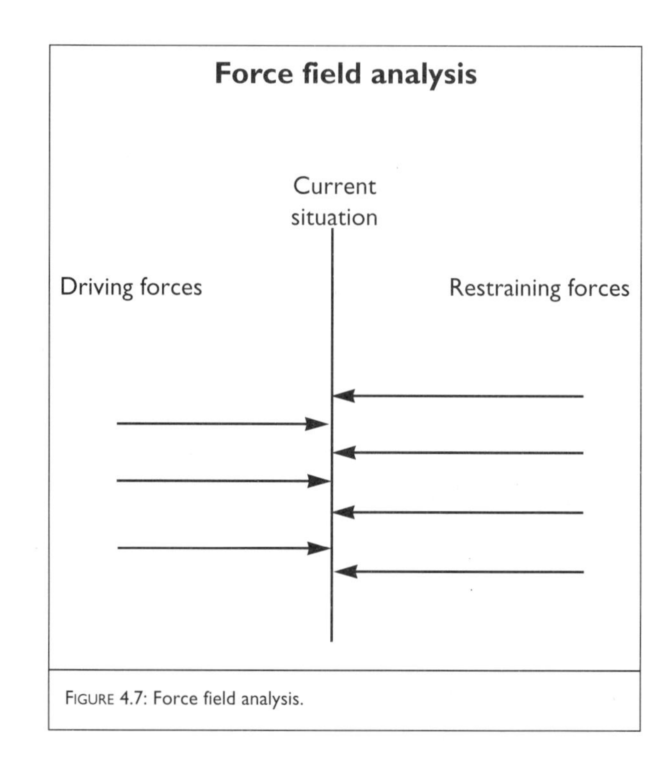

FIGURE 4.7: Force field analysis.

In *Fig. 4.7* you can take one of three actions to alter the situation:

- **increase the strength of a driving force, or add another new driving force;**
- **reduce the strength of a restraining force or remove it completely;**
- **change the direction of a force – make a restraining force into a driving force.**

For an organisational change, the forces originate from:

- **technological sources;**
- **organisational sources;**
- **external sources;**
- **individual sources.**

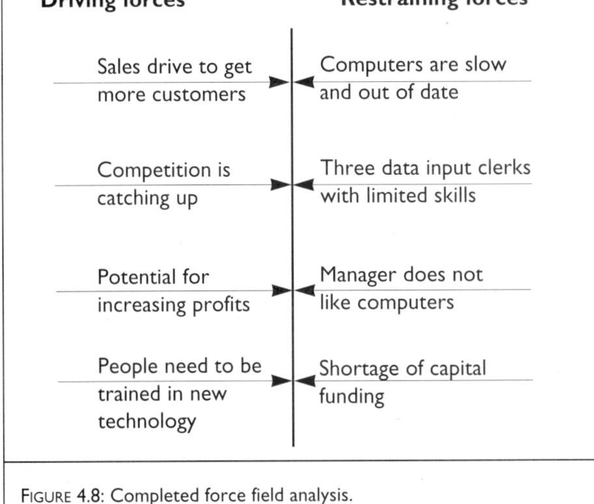

FIGURE 4.8: Completed force field analysis.

ACTIVITY

1. **In the example in *Fig. 4.8*, which of the forces do you think is the strongest?**
2. **What might be the effect of changing each force? For example, the sales drive might alter the balance by producing more customers.**
3. **Consider each force and decide upon the minimum change that might solve the problem.**

You may notice that work needs to be done on one or more force – that is called 'unfreezing'. While it is unfreezed, you can 'move' it, and then 'refreeze' it.

DEVELOPING AN IMPLEMENTATION STRATEGY

In order to ensure that changes are implemented with minimum social impact, the change plan should clearly set out to reduce resistance. To do this:

- **make information available on how the change will affect people from the beginning – a person who understands social impacts should be on the change design team;**
- **in communicating the change, encourage people to ask questions about its likely impact on them personally;**
- **where guarantees can honestly be given, communicate information about job security, job transfer, retraining, work groups, etc;**
- **obtain people's participation at the planning stage if possible, but social information must be made available as well as technical information;**
- **communicate in language that is clear to the recipients – avoid jargon that excludes some people;**
- **do not make people feel guilty by justifying the change 'because of their inefficiency' – if this approach is taken, to accept the change, people must admit they were wrong – and they will resist that;**
- **promote the change as continuing improvements on a good base – make people feel good about themselves.**

Time spent planning changes in this way is a good investment. All these strategies are available to every manager. The skill is to pick the ones that best suit the situation. The manager's objective should be to make all changes quickly with least waste of time and money.

ACTIVITY

Working in groups of three, use a force field analysis to consider a change relating to your school or college. For example, you might consider changing to a four-term year.

1 Use a large sheet of paper to record the current situation, the driving forces and the restraining forces. You may wish to interview some members of staff or students to understand the dynamics. Consider technological, organisational, external and individual sources.

2 When you have completed this, consider which forces can most easily be changed to allow the change to happen.

3 Now prepare an outline implementation plan that sets out to minimise resistance. Use the bullet point list above to guide your plan.

4 Present your findings to the whole class and be prepared to answer their questions. There will be some resistance!

PORTFOLIO ASSIGNMENT

This assignment is in two parts. The first part seeks information about job roles and the second part relates to managing change. It is based on the case study about Prodon Electronics Limited. It requires you to analyse the company and to write a business report.

Before starting the assignment, read the case study carefully. Make notes about the main issues it raises, and discuss it in depth with your colleagues so that you have a complete understanding of the situation it describes.

Prodon Electronics Limited

Jane Tomlinson is the chairperson of Prodon Electronics Limited. In her annual report, she said that 1995 had been an exceptionally good year all round. Profits had risen by 19 per cent and a dividend of 13p had been paid. She praised her colleagues on the board of directors for their strategic skills and foresight in seeing the company through the recession without harm. She singled out the new managing director in particular for praise.

The market for Prodon's products is buoyant. As interest rates have fallen, people have had more money to spend. The company is planning to expand its UK market share in the next three years from 9 per cent to 12 per cent. At the same time, it will take its first steps in establishing a foothold in mainland Europe by setting up distribution agreements with firms in Germany, Italy and Spain. From these three bases, it is intended to reach markets in all the countries of the European Union. Jane Tomlinson complimented the marketing manager and his sales team for their imaginative approach at a time when Prodon's competitors were running for cover.

Four new products are being developed, two to be introduced each year over the next two years. This will maintain Prodon's reputation of being the most innovative and forward-looking company in its sector of the industry.

This growth strategy – for increased sales and new products – will be achieved by replacing the present labour-intensive production machinery with state-of-the-art technology. Plans are being developed to increase production capacity by 25 per cent and reduce unit costs by 18 per cent through economies of scale. This will require changes throughout the organisation.

The chairperson reassured all staff that this transition will be achieved without causing hardship to those who might be affected. She complimented the production manager, his supervisors and particularly the operators who had worked with old and unreliable machines for many years without letting quality suffer. She and her board colleagues would always hold them in the highest regard.

The investment in new production technology and new product development will be financed from reserves. Steps are underway to offer shares to all staff at discounted rates to allow them to enjoy the prosperity generated by their hard work. She expressed her thanks to the finance manager and the personnel manager for working closely together to produce a very attractive scheme in which all staff, from directors to operators, have the same opportunity to benefit. The finance and personnel managers – and their staff – had played a key part in maintaining efficiency and keeping overheads under control.

Jane Tomlinson concluded her chairperson's report by announcing a major reassessment of employment policy together with an extensive retraining programme. This will give staff the opportunity to upgrade their skills and enjoy greater job satisfaction in the new high-technology environment. She thanked all the staff for their dedicated service and said she looked forward to continuing prosperity for Prodon Electronics, with all staff sharing its fruits.

The report's content is specified in task 2 and 4. It should follow a standard business report format. It should be word processed and spell-checked. Try to make it a professional piece of work.

Task 1

This task sets out the work you have to do to analyse job roles and responsibilities.

(a) When you have a clear understanding of the case study, draw a diagram which shows the likely organisation structure of Prodon Electronics. It should identify all the job roles referred to in the case study.

(b) Draw a grid on a big piece of paper, with six columns and five rows. The amount of space available for each box should be enough to write 30-50 words. Leave the box in the top left-hand corner blank. Then, in the first column, down the left hand side of your grid, write the job roles you have identified from the case study. In the first row, at the top of your grid, write the following duties:

- identifying and meeting targets;
- working with others;
- training;
- discipline;
- implementing change.

(c) Write brief notes in the appropriate boxes about the responsibilities each role-holder in Prodon has for each of the duties listed at the top of the grid. For example, briefly note what are a director's responsibilities for 'identifying and meeting targets'. Then do the same for each of the other roles, highlighting the differences between the roles. These notes are the raw material for your business report.

Task 2

Now you should write part one of your business report. Using the notes you made in task 1, write a report on the job roles and responsibilities at Prodon Electronics.

(a) Explain the different job roles you have identified in Prodon Electronics.

(b) Set out in an orderly and easily understandable fashion, the responsibilities of each role for each of the five duties listed in task 1.

Task 3

Now you should consider the management of change. The case study contains direct reference to some important changes that are being planned at Prodon. There are also some implied changes; for example, at one point it notes that 'this will require changes throughout the organisation'.

(a) Identify and list all the changes, express and implied, referred to in the case study. Where several changes are closely related, you may wish to classify them under common headings. See, for example, the classification on page 32. You may use other classifications if you prefer.

(b) Make notes that briefly explain why Prodon must make each of these changes. In addition, select one of the changes that relates to working conditions and make detailed notes that explain in depth the reasons for that change.

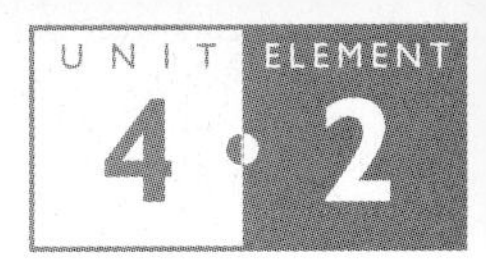

(c) Prodon's chairperson shows a great understanding of the reasons that people fear and resist change. Make notes of the things she said that are intended to lessen resistance.

(d) Develop a force field analysis to help you understand the dynamics of any one of the changes you identified above. Use your overall knowledge of business studies to identify 'forces'. Be imaginative and do not be constrained by tradition or convention.

(e) Develop an implementation plan based on the force field analysis, and on the need to minimise resistance. Identify the job roles which would be involved at each stage of the implementation, and state their responsibilities during the implementation.

TASK 4

Drawing on the work you undertook in Task 3, write the second part of your report.

(a) Explain briefly why a range of changes are necessary in business.

(b) Give a detailed explanation of one reason why working conditions change.

(c) Illustrate and explain a strategy for implementing a change to working conditions.

(d) Explain the responsibilities of different levels of job roles at different stages of the implementation.

Evaluate recruitment procedures, job applications and interviews

Getting the right people in the right jobs is fundamental to the success of an organisation.

If an unsuitable person is employed, the organisation will either become less efficient or managers will have to go through the whole selection process again. That would be an expensive waste of valuable management time.

In this element, we examine the process of finding the right person for the job by a series of short activities based on the following scenario.

The personnel manager

Imagine you are the personnel manager of a company making and distributing pharmaceuticals.

Working quietly in your office, you are interrupted by the sales office manager. She is flustered and irate: 'I'm fed up with the quality of sales staff we get nowadays. Can't the personnel department do something about it? Our newer recruits want to be spoon-fed, they want to have no work to do and to be paid a fortune for not doing it!'

Concerned at her frustration, you suggest that she sits down and has a cup of coffee while you discuss the problem. Once she has calmed down, you try to consider the problem rationally.

'What we've got to do,' you say, 'is to examine our recruitment and selection process, so that it helps us to choose people who can do the job we want, to the standard we want, and to fit in with our existing team.'

The sales office manager agrees, but adds doubtfully, 'if there is such a process.'

The recruitment process

Sadly, there is no foolproof way of guaranteeing success. However, *Fig. 4.9* (on page 42) illustrates a well tried-and-tested process that reduces the risk of selecting the wrong person for a job.

Copy *Fig. 4.9* into your notes. It is quite like a 'map' that shows a logical route to a destination. (It is, in fact, called a **process map**.) The destination in this case is 'employing competent people'. The logical approach is important – it ensures that information is gathered in the right order, that it is relevant for its purpose, and that the conclusion is based on sound reasons.

Now we will look at each step in turn so that we have a full understanding of how it works.

Job analysis

Creating a new post, or replacing someone who has left, gives a manager an opportunity to analyse the job that has to be done. Rather than just 'replace' the person who has left the post, it is often a chance to consider other (and perhaps better) ways of getting the work done.

- **The job may have changed** gradually over the years and no longer warrants a full-time appointment.
- **The departing person** may have 'bent' the job slightly to suit his or her own strengths. This might have resulted in important parts of the job not being done properly.
- **The manager** should consider whether the work could be reorganised – perhaps shared among existing staff; or even moved to another department.
- **There may be alternatives to a full-time position,** such as employing a part-timer, using temporary 'agency' staff or through more overtime by existing staff.
- **The use of more up-to-date technology** should be considered.

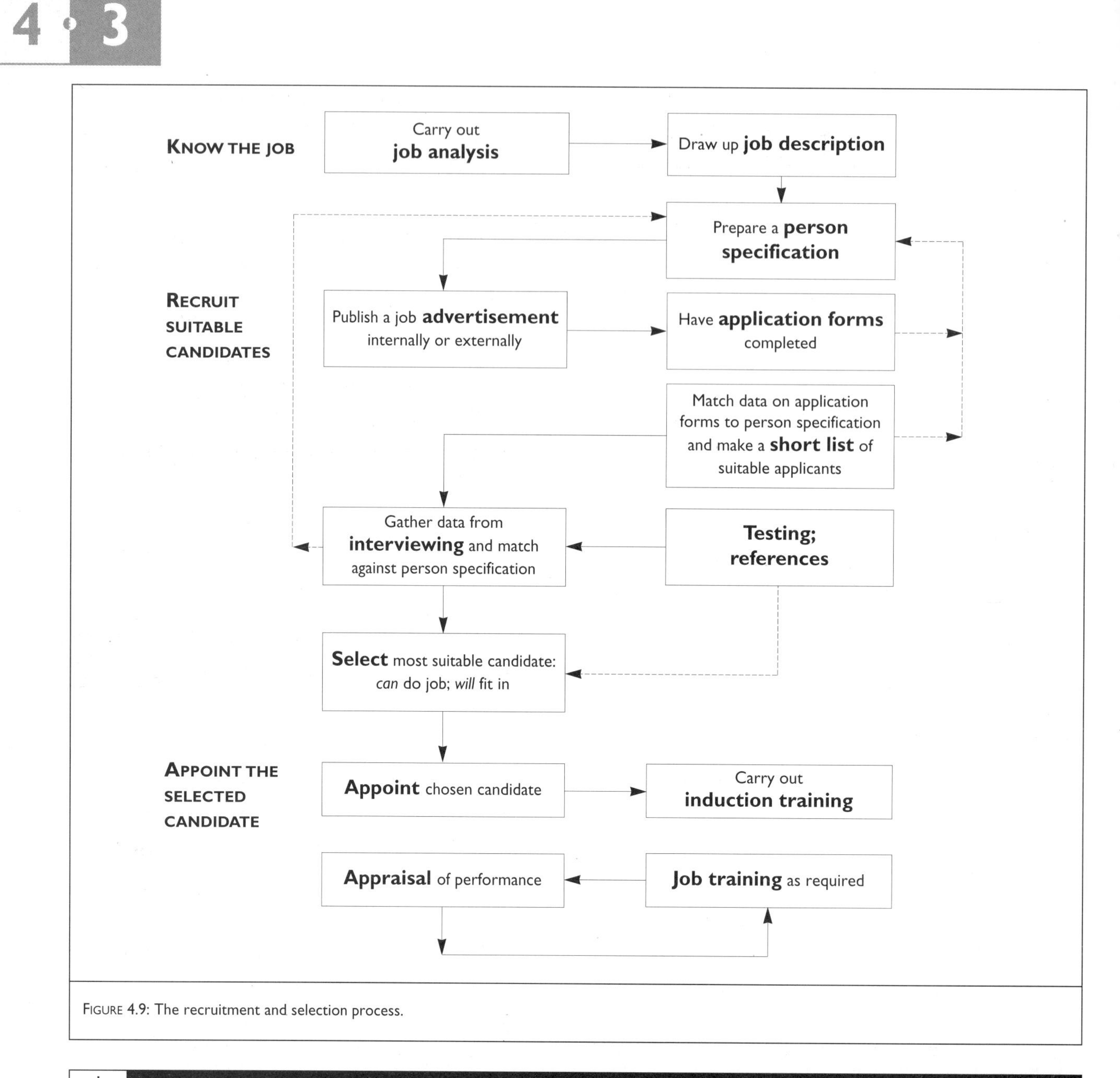

FIGURE 4.9: The recruitment and selection process.

ACTIVITY

1 Read through the list of considerations about filling a vacant post given on page 41. Try to add other ways of getting work done that do not involve full-time staff. Be imaginative and innovative. For example, consider the options that are opened up by sub-contracting particular work to another business to carry out for you; or the wider use of information technology that, for example, allows people to work from home.

2 Prepare some notes on how technology might change the types of jobs that will be available in the future.

3 Form a small discussion group of up to (say) five colleagues. Use the notes you have made to contribute constructively to a discussion on 'job opportunities in the next century' with your class colleagues. After the discussion, list all the ways you have thought of to get work done.

The simplest and most common methods of analysing jobs are:

- **questioning the job holder;**
- **observing the job holder at work.**

The information gathered is carefully recorded and analysed. Usually the job holder's manager is able to give additional information, although it tends to be rather general and would not normally be sufficient on its own. There are several other ways in which jobs can be analysed, but they are beyond the scope of this book.

In our scenario (see page 41), it might be a good idea for the sales office manager to consider exactly what the job of 'sales staff' entails. She needs to be absolutely clear about the tasks that the job holder will have to perform and the standard of work required.

She should describe the responsibilities of the job by answering the following questions:

- **what tasks have to be completed by the job holder?**
- **how often is each task done and how important is it?**
- **is there technology involved that requires special skills?**
- **what mental processes are required to do the job?**
- **is the job holder required to take decisions and use initiative?**
- **if so, what are the limits of his or her authority?**
- **is the output from the job a part or a whole?**
- **does the job holder have to work with others, or control the work of others?**
- **what are the required performance standards and how are they measured?**

ACTIVITY

Some of your colleagues work in shops and supermarkets in the evenings and at weekends. Form a group of three or four, and make sure that at least one of the group works in a shop.

Use the nine questions above to establish the responsibilities of that person's job. Keep your notes.

JOB DESCRIPTIONS

When all this information has been gathered by the job analyst, it should be written down in a summary report setting out what the job entails. This summary report is normally called a **job description**. It contains two types of information: it describes the **tasks** of the job and it describes the **behaviour** necessary to actually do the tasks satisfactorily.

When the sales office manager in our scenario has completed the analysis, she should write a job description. This information is most valuable in trying to decide what sort of person might be able to do the job satisfactorily. *Fig 4.10* (on page 44) shows how a job description for her salesperson might look.

Job Description

Name of post:	Salesperson
Responsible to:	Sales office manager
Responsible for:	No direct staff
Relationships with:	Sales clerks; warehouse personnel; customers.
Job summary:	To call upon existing and potential customers according to the prescribed call schedule. To collect repeat orders, introduce new lines, open new accounts, arrange deliveries and returns, and collect overdue accounts. Keep customer records.
Job responsibilities:	The salesperson is responsible for selling the company's range of pharmaceuticals. He or she must know and keep up to date with the complete range of goods so as to inform and advise chemists of latest developments. He or she must behave in a professional manner and exercise care and security with samples and products. He or she must deal sensitively with complaints and errors. He or she must follow schedules and report daily on shortfalls.
Working conditions:	The salesperson will drive a company van, keep it clean and roadworthy, and ensure that any accidents or faults are reported immediately to the sales office manager.
Standards:	All calls must be made to schedule. Complaints and errors must be dealt with within 24 hours. Orders must be processed on the day they are taken. Records must be completed immediately after call. Sales targets must be met.

FIGURE 4.10: Job description for a salesperson.

ACTIVITY

Study the job description for a salesperson. Try to visualise a salesperson visiting a customer and carrying out the duties described.

Pick out and list the key tasks that a salesperson would be expected to do. Against each key task write two questions you could ask a job applicant. Your questions should be designed so that the applicant's answers will indicate whether he or she is competent to do that task to the required standard.

This is a difficult exercise, but one that interviewers have to do. So test out your questions on a colleague who has also studied the job description. Do they produce answers that show competence?

PERSON SPECIFICATION

A **person specification** (sometimes called a **personnel profile**) describes the characteristics and attributes which a person would need to be able to do the job to the required standards.

There are several ways of setting out this information. The one we will use is called the **seven point plan**. It simply describes the person you are looking for under seven broad headings. These headings are:

- **physical make-up** – what should the person look and sound like?
- **attainments** – what education, qualifications and experience should the person have?
- **general intelligence** – what intellectual capacity should the person have?
- **special aptitudes** – what special skills and talents are needed by the person?
- **interests** – what sort of pastimes or hobbies would the ideal person follow?
- **disposition** – what motivation and temperament and attitude should the person have?
- **circumstances** – what personal and domestic arrangements and location might the ideal person have?

Using this seven point plan, *Fig. 4.11* illustrates the person specification for a salesperson.

Physical make-up
Well groomed; smartly dressed.
Clear grammatical speech.

Attainments
Four GCSEs grade C, including chemistry or a science. Formal sales training preferred. Clean driving licence.

General intelligence
Above average. Quick on the uptake. Agile mind.

Special aptitudes
Ability to listen. High in social skills. Accuracy and clear handwriting.

Interests
Any team sport or social responsibility.

Disposition
Pleasant and happy. Ability to cope with customers who are upset.

Circumstances
Preferred stable, settled home life. Able to work occasional Saturdays. Lives on territory.

FIGURE 4.11: Person specification for a salesperson.

ACTIVITY

1 Do you agree that the characteristics listed in *Fig. 4.11* are appropriate for a salesperson? Justify your evaluation.

2 How might these characteristics differ if, instead, you want to recruit a computer programmer or an accounts clerk?

There is a certain similarity between a person specification and a photofit picture used by the police in hunting suspects. The police gather information, analyse it and come up with an idea of what the offender might look like. The difference is that we are hunting for an ideal employee who will help to make our business prosper, and not someone who will 'rob' us by failing to do the job to the required standard.

FINDING SUITABLE CANDIDATES

The next stage of the recruitment process is to attract people who fit the company's person specification, and no others. The first task is to identify, accurately, where the ideal people can be found. They may be found within the company itself, but doing a different job; they may be found through the families and friends of present staff. However, it might be necessary to advertise the position more widely. In which case, it is important to think about the type of people that the company is trying to attract and the publications they read:

- **they may be readers of the *Daily Telegraph* or the *Daily Mirror*;**
- **if the post is a very technical one, or is highly specialised, there are specialist journals which are read by the people suitable for these posts;**
- **if someone straight from school or college, or on a youth training programme, would be ideal, the company may want to contact the careers service;**
- **for specialist and management jobs, the most popular medium for advertising is the relevant professional and trade press.**

The sales office manager in our scenario has the task now of deciding how to communicate her job needs in such a way as to attract suitable candidates. Let us not forget, the problem which she is trying to solve is that her 'newer recruits' are unsuitable. This is her chance to use carefully worded advertisements or notices to attract really suitable candidates.

Research suggests that there are four things that most applicants look for in a job advertisement. They are:

- **details about the organisation – who would I be working for?**
- **a clear description of the job – what would I be doing?**
- **the location – where would I be doing it?**
- **the salary scale – what financial reward would I get?**

The advertisement should also make it quite clear how any interested person should apply. Our sales office manager may decide to ask for a curriculum vitae (CV). Or she may simply ask them to write or phone for an application form.

JOB ADVERTISEMENTS

Advertising can be expensive. A national daily can charge over £80 per single column centimetre each time an advertisement is run.

ACTIVITY

Calculate the price of an advertisement two columns wide and 15cm long in a newspaper that charges £70 per single column centimetre. How much would it cost if you published it three times?

If you publish four times, you will get a discount of 20 per cent off all four advertisements. Which option would you choose, and why?

A business wants a good return on its investment on advertising, so it makes good business sense to write a clear, precise advertisement that will attract the right sort of people. It seems sensible for a company to provide the four pieces of essential information in its job advertisements.

In drafting advertisements, employers must respect the laws that relate to employment and recrutiment.

- **The Disabled Persons (Employment) Act 1944 and 1958** provides that an employer of more than twenty people has a duty to employ a quota of disabled people.
- **The Equal Pay Act 1970** requires that equal pay is given for work of equal value.
- **The Sex Discrimination Acts 1975 and 1986** make it unlawful to discriminate against persons, directly or indirectly, on the grounds of race, gender or marital status.
- **The Race Relations Act 1976** requires that equal access to jobs and promotion is provided to people of equal ability irrespective of race, colour or creed.
- **The Employment Act 1990** makes it unlawful to discriminate against union members in a job advertisement.

The penalty for a breach of these laws can be severe. Courts can impose heavy fines and companies have to meet the legal costs involved. In addition, it costs management time in answering any charges, there is stress imposed upon those managers who must give evidence in the courts, and court cases can attract a lot of adverse publicity.

ACTIVITY

Using the two advertisements shown in *Fig. 4.12* as a guide, design an advertisement for the job of salesperson. Make sure that your advertisement incorporates the four main points above that people look for in an advertisement, and that it stays within the law. If there is information you need for the advertisement that has not been given to you, just use your imagination and invent it.

FIGURE 4.12: Award winning job advertisements.

Application forms

The purpose of an application form is to gather information about the candidate that will give definite clues about personal attributes, qualifications, experience and so on.

By matching the information given on the application form (or in a curriculum vitae) with the person specification, it should be possible to decide on a shortlist of the most suitable applicants. These should be invited to attend an interview.

The remaining applicants should each receive a letter thanking them for their application, but explaining that they are not successful on this occasion. Managers and other executives are busy people. Interviewing unsuitable people both unnecessarily raises their expectations and wastes valuable management time.

The completed application form of the selected candidate will form part of the contract of employment. Any deliberate misinformation could render the contract void, resulting in dismissal.

Curriculum vitae

A curriculum vitae (CV) is a document usually initiated and prepared by a job seeker. It serves a similar purpose to an application form. It supplies a prospective employer with the job seeker's details. It should include information on:

- **personal details;**
- **education;**
- **qualifications;**
- **work experience;**
- **interests;**
- **ambitions.**

Choosing the best person

The stages of the recruitment process that we have been studying so far have been designed to achieve two things: to determine precisely the sort of person needed to do the job to the required standard and then to attract such people to apply for the job.

The next stage is to gather information about each applicant. The information should allow the business to choose the best person for the job. We consider five ways of doing this:

- **application forms or CVs;**
- **interviews;**
- **testing;**
- **taking references;**
- **assessment centres.**

Standard Application Form (SAF) Please complete this form in BLACK ink or typescript. AGCAS/AGR approved form Check employer literature or vacancy information for correct application procedure.				Name of Employer	
Current/most recent University/College				Vacancies or training schemes for which you wish to apply Job function(s) Location(s)	
First name (BLOCK LETTERS) Out of term address (BLOCK LETTERS): give dates at this address Postcode Telephone				Surname (Dr, Mr, Mrs, Miss, Ms) (BLOCK LETTERS) Term address (BLOCK LETTERS) give dates of address Postcode Telephone	
Date of birth	Age	Country of birth		Nationality/Citizenship	Do you need a work permit to take up employment in the UK?
Secondary/Further Education Name of School(s)/College(s)	From	To		Subjects /courses studied and level (eg GCSE, O, A, AS,H, IB, BTEC, GNVQ) Give examination results with grades and dates	
First degree/diploma University/College	From	To	Degree/diploma (BA, HND, etc.)	Class expected/ obtained	Title of degree/ diploma course
Main subjects with examination results or course grades to date, if known					
Postgraduate qualifications University/College	From	To	PhD/MA/ Diploma etc.	Title of research topic or course Supervisor	

FIGURE 4.13: A standard application form.

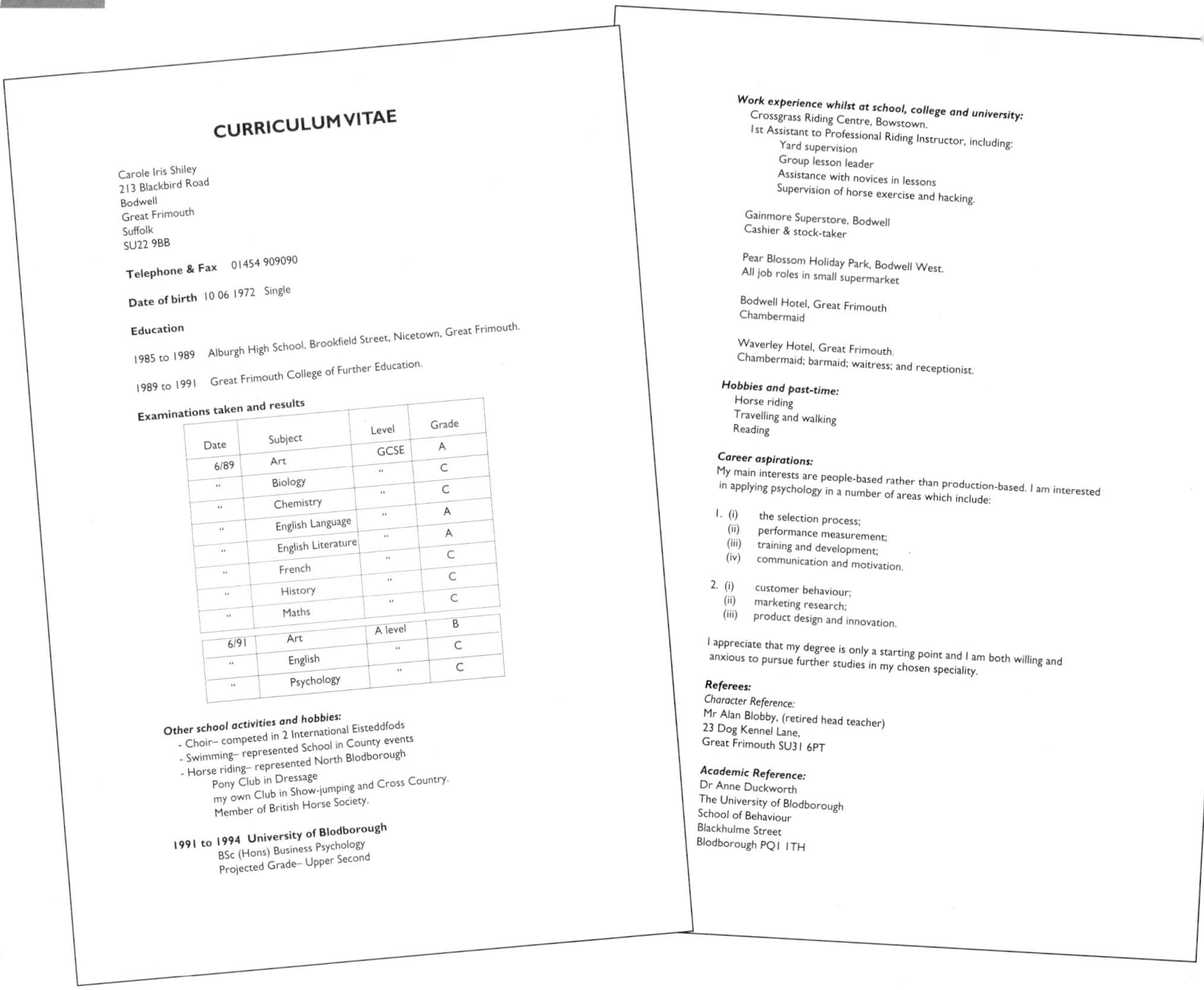

CURRICULUM VITAE

Carole Iris Shiley
213 Blackbird Road
Bodwell
Great Frimouth
Suffolk
SU22 9BB

Telephone & Fax 01454 909090

Date of birth 10 06 1972 Single

Education

1985 to 1989 Alburgh High School, Brookfield Street, Nicetown, Great Frimouth.

1989 to 1991 Great Frimouth College of Further Education.

Examinations taken and results

Date	Subject	Level	Grade
6/89	Art	GCSE	A
"	Biology	"	C
"	Chemistry	"	C
"	English Language	"	A
"	English Literature	"	A
"	French	"	C
"	History	"	C
"	Maths	"	C
6/91	Art	A level	B
"	English	"	C
"	Psychology	"	C

Other school activities and hobbies:
- Choir– competed in 2 International Eisteddfods
- Swimming– represented School in County events
- Horse riding– represented North Blodborough
  Pony Club in Dressage
  my own Club in Show-jumping and Cross Country.
  Member of British Horse Society.

1991 to 1994 University of Blodborough
BSc (Hons) Business Psychology
Projected Grade– Upper Second

Work experience whilst at school, college and university:
Crossgrass Riding Centre, Bowstown.
1st Assistant to Professional Riding Instructor, including:
Yard supervision
Group lesson leader
Assistance with novices in lessons
Supervision of horse exercise and hacking.

Gainmore Superstore, Bodwell
Cashier & stock-taker

Pear Blossom Holiday Park, Bodwell West.
All job roles in small supermarket

Bodwell Hotel, Great Frimouth
Chambermaid

Waverley Hotel, Great Frimouth.
Chambermaid; barmaid; waitress; and receptionist.

Hobbies and past-time:
Horse riding
Travelling and walking
Reading

Career aspirations:
My main interests are people-based rather than production-based. I am interested in applying psychology in a number of areas which include:

1. (i) the selection process;
   (ii) performance measurement;
   (iii) training and development;
   (iv) communication and motivation.

2. (i) customer behaviour;
   (ii) marketing research;
   (iii) product design and innovation.

I appreciate that my degree is only a starting point and I am both willing and anxious to pursue further studies in my chosen speciality.

Referees:
Character Reference:
Mr Alan Blobby, (retired head teacher)
23 Dog Kennel Lane,
Great Frimouth SU31 6PT

Academic Reference:
Dr Anne Duckworth
The University of Blodborough
School of Behaviour
Blackhulme Street
Blodborough PQ1 1TH

Figure 4.14: A curriculum vitae.

In addition, the CV should include any other information that would be likely to persuade a prospective employer to consider granting an interview. It should also offer at least two referees who will corroborate what has been claimed – one should be a character reference and the other a work reference.

A CV should provide a pen picture of the values and skills a job seeker can bring to any prospective employer. The job seeker hopes that it will result in an interview at which he or she can further illustrate how valuable he or she could be to the business.

SELECTION INTERVIEWS

An interview can be described as a planned discussion with a specific purpose. Interviews are used in many different circumstances for many different purposes. Although we are only concerned with selection here, it is worth noting that interviews are used in appraisal, counselling, grievance and disciplinary procedures.

A selection interview is a mutual exchange of information. As well as allowing a company to find out about the applicants, it is an opportunity to give applicants as much information about the job as possible, so that they can decide whether or not they want to take the job if it is offered. Nearly 40 per cent of candidates who are made job offers do not take them up.

A company wants people who accept jobs to be motivated to work for the business. Treating them with respect at an interview is an opportunity to start nurturing this motivation. It is important that all applicants are treated in a way that is seen to be legal, fair and just.

RELIABILITY OF INTERVIEWS

There is a great deal of research evidence to show that interviewing is a very inexact process. Many researchers have shown that, given exactly the same information, different interviewers form very different opinions of the same candidate.

Some research conducted in 1964 by E C Webster of McGill University, Canada, provides some interesting conclusions that are as valid today as then.

- **Interviewers'** first impressions arise from the application form and from their first sight of the interviewee. Evidence shows that they seldom change their opinion of the candidate based on these first impressions.
- **Interviewers** make their decision about a candidate in the first few minutes of the interview, then spend the rest of the interview gathering evidence to support this initial decision.
- **Most interviewers** tend to look for reasons why candidates are *not* suitable rather than look for evidence that they *are* suitable
- **If an interviewer** has made an early decision, this is communicated to the candidate by the interviewer's body language, and the interviewee will respond accordingly.

Despite these serious weaknesses, which are reasonably well established, interviewing is still the most common selection technique used by businesses today.

Preparing the interview questions

The interviewer's questions should be designed to get the candidates to talk about their work experiences and their lives in general. These are called 'open questions'. Answers to open questions can reveal clues as to whether interviewees can do the job, whether they are motivated, and give some indication of how they cope in a variety of situations – including those where they are likely to be under pressure and stress.

The novelist and poet, Rudyard Kipling, showed how to ask open questions when he wrote:

> ***I keep six honest serving-men***
> ***(They taught me all I knew);***
> ***Their names are What and Why and When***
> ***And How and Where and Who.***

Words like what, why, when and how help to keep questions open. A question like 'how did you do your stocktaking' invites a very different answer from 'did you do stocktaking'. Phrases such as 'tell me about ...' or 'can you explain ...' should produce answers that give a great deal of useful information. Questions should not imply the answer. They should not invite a 'yes' or 'no' answer. For example, 'I expect you were very busy in your job' will almost certainly get the answer 'oh yes, I was'. It is of little or no use.

Where an applicant's answer leaves doubt, or raises an interesting issue, it should be probed further. A response like 'I was responsible for the stock' may mean that the candidate kept the records up to date, or it could mean that full budget responsibility rested on that person's shoulders.

Two important interviewing skills are **probing for clues** and **active listening**. If interviewees are to reveal their ability, experience, and motivation, they, not the interviewer, must do most of the talking. The interviewer should aim to let the interviewee speak for at least 60 per cent of the interview. That is quite difficult for the interviewer to achieve without careful preparation.

It is important to avoid asking any questions that may discriminate against a person or group of people. It is illegal to ask 'do you intend to start a family'.

The interview

Besides giving careful consideration to the questions that they will have to ask in order to assess interviewees' suitability for the job, the interviewer has to do other preparation.

If an interviewee is to relax and be open with the interviewer, there should be a conducive atmosphere. Comfortable chairs should be arranged to avoid barriers between the interviewer and interviewee, to allow eye contact and to allow the interviewer to use body language to remove threats from a tense situation.

It is also good manners to arrange a warm welcome for the interviewees, to take coats and hang them up, and to offer them somewhere to freshen up before the interview starts. It is also respectful to arrange that there should be no interruptions during the interview.

Before the start of the interview, all documents about the interviewees should be gathered and read again so that their details are fresh in the interviewer's mind.

Interviews should follow a structure. There are many ways of structuring an interview. Here is one suggestion:

- **tell the interviewee** how the interview will be structured;
- **then, tell the interviewee** about the job so that he or she can apply their answers to the actual job;
- **answer any questions** the interviewee has about the job;
- **ask planned questions,** taking care to avoid illegal questions;
- **listen to the answers** (remember the 60 per cent/40 per cent rule) and take notes discretely;
- **through follow-up questions,** probe and develop issues that arise during the answers to planned questions;
- **maintain** a brisk, businesslike tempo;
- **conclude the interview** with a clear summary, and a statement of what will happen next and when.

The whole process is a commentary on the organisation's culture – interviewees will take away an impression of the business and its values. This will influence whether they want to take the job if selected.

Types of interview

There are a number of ways of organising selection interviews. The most common are:

- **one-to-one interviews;**
- **successive interviews;**
- **tandem interviews;**
- **panel interviews.**

In **one-to-one interviews**, one trained interviewer conducts all the interviews and selects the most appropriate applicant. The one-to-one interview is popular because it demands less management time, and is preferred by most interviewees. They seem to cope more easily when they need only relate to one person, and where the questions follow a logical pattern.

This process can be extended so that the candidate has successive interviews with different managers. It has been found that candidates tend to become bored with **successive interviews** and, sometimes, they become better at answering questions as the interviews proceed. It also takes a lot of their time.

In **tandem interviews**, a firm uses a line manager in tandem with a personnel specialist in the hope that each brings special knowledge and skill to the situation. This can be economical, acceptable and an efficient use of time.

Panel interviews are often used in the public sector. Up to five people sit on a panel and the candidate is interviewed once only, but by the whole panel. For most people, this is a daunting experience. It is more like a tribunal sitting in judgement than an interview.

ACTIVITY

In view of the past experiences of the sales office manager in selecting unsuitable people, which type of interview would you recommend?

Which person (or persons) should conduct the interviews? If more than one person is involved, what role should each interviewer play?

Explain why you think your choice might be more successful in getting the right sort of people.

Evaluating interviews

A simple way to monitor a person's interviewing skills is to use a check list (see *Fig. 4.15*). The difficulty with having a person evaluating during an actual interview is that it might add pressure and cause the interviewees not to give of their best.

Interview check list

Name of interviewer

A	B	C

Grade each of the following points 1 to 10 as follows:

0 1 2 3 4 5 6 7 8 9 10

Needs a lot of improvement — Acceptable standard (average) — Excellent could not be improved upon

Items	A	B	C
Preparation:			
1. Room layout/ arrangement			
2. All documents to hand			
3. Clear knowledge of:			
job description			
personnel profile			
application form			
4. Appropriate questions prepared for points to be investigated			

Items	A	B	C
Interview			
5. Was applicant put at ease?			
6. Was 'purpose' clearly explained?			
7. Was 'structure' clear?			
8. Talk ratio? Applicant? %			
9. Did interview follow a pattern?			
10. Use of open questions?			
11. Were issues 'followed'?			
12. Were 'gaps' in history investigated?			
13. Any long digressions?			
14. Brisk tempo? (Business like?)			
15. Clear summary?			
16. Notes taken unobtrusively?			

FIGURE 4.15: Interview check list.

TESTING

Besides being an inexact process, interviewing may not give enough information about various aspects of an applicant's ability, experience and personality. Additional data can be gathered by different types of test.

Some people consider testing an invasion of privacy, others simply doubt its value. However, if tests are to be used, there is a strong moral obligation on the user to ensure that the tests chosen are valid and reliable for the purpose for which they are used. They should be conducted by a person who is competent, trained and qualified (some require that the user holds a licence) in their use and the interpretation of the data collected.

Tests must be valid – that is, they must test what they are intended to test. Otherwise the test cannot be described as a valid predictor of successful job

performance. Tests must be reliable – that is, they must be consistent in measuring what they are supposed to measure whenever they are repeated.

Types of test

Aptitude tests are tests which are designed to show that an applicant has the basic mental and physical qualities required for success in a particular job. They are often used to help a business select people who have no previous experience of a particular job (such as new apprentices). A business that invests in training apprentices is taking less of a selection risk if it uses an appropriate aptitude test, than if it does not use any.

Achievement and **attainment tests** are used to measure skills already learned. For example, people applying for a secretarial post may be asked to do a typing test. All applicants that achieve the required standard in the test are considered further; those that do not are rejected.

Intelligence tests measure a person's intelligence quotient (IQ). People whose scores fall below a known minimum IQ for the job being filled would not be interviewed. It is important that intelligence tests are used precisely as directed, and they should always be given under the control of a psychologist.

Personality tests assess a person's emotional make-up. They attempt to predict an individual's behaviour under different circumstances. Personality is described by plotting an individual's score on a series of factors.

One of the most popular is the **Cattell Sixteen Personality Factor Test** (16PF). *Fig. 4.16* shows a completed chart for six of Cattell's factors.

Serious	□	□	□	□	□	□	□	X	□	Outgoing
Affected by feelings	□	X	□	□	□	□	□	□	□	Emotionally unstable
Submissive	□	□	□	□	□	□	□	X	□	Dominant
Group dependent	□	□	□	□	X	□	□	□	□	Self-sufficient
Conservative	X	□	□	□	□	□	□	□	□	Experimenting
Trusting	□	□	□	□	□	□	X	□	□	Suspicious

FIGURE 4.16: Sample of a result of Cattell Sixteen Personality Factor Test.

To take the test, a candidate completes a questionnaire which, when analysed by the expert, shows where he or she falls on each of the scales. For example, the individual shown on the scale in *Fig 4.16* is very outgoing, emotional, very dominant, quite self-sufficient, very conservative and quite suspicious.

ACTIVITY

1 Would any of the tests we have discussed add useful information to help our sales office manager improve selection? If so, what type of test do you think would be helpful?

2 Let us assume that you decide to use a personality test. You have asked some consultants to carry it out for you and they have quoted a fee of £3,500. They do not guarantee that the test will assure success in selection, but they assure you that they will identify anyone who is unlikely to be successful. Write a memo to the financial director justifying the expenditure. Your memo should outline the financial advantages of 'making the right choice first time'.

References

A reference is an opinion, usually in writing, of a person's character, ability, honesty and reliability in support of a job application.

The problem with references is that it is usually impossible to obtain a detailed and accurate report from their current employers on how candidates are performing in their present jobs.

- **It would be unethical** to contact a present employer who may not be aware that an employee had applied for another job.

- **Some employers do give references** to current employees, for example, teachers and local government staff can get references from their current employers, but it is hard to know if these are accurate and unbiased.

- **Personal relationships** can influence some referees more than job performance, even to the extent of writing a glowing reference to get rid of someone they do not like!

Past employers are often cautious when writing references. There is no legal obligation to provide references on request, but most employers do. References must be accurate. Any fake information, or any omissions

> ## Employers 'must take care' on job references
>
> The legal scales tipped in favour of job hunters yesterday when the House of Lords ruled that employers have a duty to take reasonable care when writing references about former staff members.
>
> The case opens the possibility of court actions against companies on the grounds that they have been negligent in assessing the conduct and behaviour of their employees, so damaging these people's chances of gaining work with other organisations.
>
> The case seems certain to lead to managers thinking more deeply about the implications of the thousands of references written every day. One effect, however, could be to encourage the practice of giving confidential references given over the telephone, making it virtually impossible for disgruntled employees to bring legal cases.
>
> Mr Morgan, director of the Industrial Society, a body promoting good employment practice, said: 'A reference can affect the rest of somebody's life, so integrity is vital. This ruling will focus employers on good practice, which is to provide references which are fair and authentic, not opinionated and anecdotal.'
>
> *Financial Times*, 8 July 1995

that might cause a candidate to fail to be offered a job which he or she would have been offered had the correct information been given, may make a case for damages against the writer of the reference.

ACTIVITY

Refer back to the material on the contract of employment in element 1 and look again at the implied terms that are read into all contracts by the courts. Can you see where this House of Lords ruling fits in?

ASSESSMENT CENTRES

Many of you seeking a career in a large or medium-sized organisation may find that the selection process is carried out by means of an **assessment centre**. Some firms, like W H Smith and English China Clay, have developed their own very successful assessment centres.

The name is a little deceiving – it is not a place. It is a series of events and activities in which all candidates for a job take part. The events are designed to provide evidence against predetermined standards of competence in specific attributes and skills. The design of assessment centres is normally carried out by occupational psychologists.

Evidence is often sought relating to skills and competence in:

- **oral and written communication;**
- **openness in dealings with others;**
- **sensitivity to other people;**
- **leadership and persuasiveness;**
- **decision-making;**
- **assertiveness.**

Note is also taken of the use of initiative, common sense, energy, ability to 'come back after a fall' and, particularly, the degree of achievement and motivation exhibited by each candidate.

Assessment is usually along a scale (say from one to eight) for each of the above criteria. One is dreadful and eight is amazing. Assessors are carefully trained in observation skills, and are drawn from human resources specialists, line managers and senior managers. There is usually one assessor for every two candidates.

The focus of the assessment centre is on peoples' strengths, in the belief that there is immediate return from exploiting a person's strengths. Weaknesses that are identified are fed back to the candidate for attention, but not in a critical way. We all have weaknesses that need to be addressed.

There is an equal opportunities issue here that must be addressed by the assessors. A solitary woman or a single individual from an ethnic minority might feel inhibited. It is for the assessors to take this into account when evaluating the participants. In fact, in most situations where this inhibition might occurs, it is common for at least one of the assessors to represent the minority group or groups.

Despite its expense and use of time, firms that use assessment centres claim that it reduces the incidence of selection errors markedly. If results are that good, then it is a wonderful investment.

ACTIVITY

Consider the ethical issues associated with selection in general, and with assessment centres in particular.

Write a short report for the human resources manager pointing out the steps you have taken to ensure that all recruitment and selection procedures are fair and offer equal opportunity to all applicants.

The report should highlight legal requirements and how they are being met.

MAKING APPPOINTMENTS

In the entire recruitment and selection process, it is illegal to set any standards, or ask for qualifications, experience or personal qualities that would discriminate unfairly against minority racial groups, the disabled or one sex. It may be important to keep a record of reasons for appointing or rejecting candidates to show that these legal obligations are being met.

The selected candidate will be offered the job and, presumably, will accept it. At this stage, the other candidates should be informed and thanked for their time and interest.

If the sales office manager in our scenario follows this process, do you think she would stand a good chance of resolving her staffing problem? If you answer 'yes' to this, would you also agree that people are worth looking after once they have joined a company?

ACTIVITY

Many people reject job offers. Assume that you are a personnel specialist who has just made an offer to the applicant who is best suited for the job requirements, but she has declined. None of the other candidates is suitable. Your managing director has just phoned to say that the vacancy must be filled quickly and you are to offer that job to one of the other applicants.

Prepare a case to put to the managing director that sets out the disadvantages of taking the route she has ordered. You should include the financial as well as the other implications. It should also include a short-term solution to the problem while you pursue a more permanent one.

ETHICAL OBLIGATIONS

As with other professions, the personnel and development profession has a ruling body – the Institute of Personnel and Development (IPD) – which sets out codes of practice which should be followed by all practitioners, whether members of the institute or not.

The institute published a code of professional conduct in 1995. This included individual codes on:

- **recruitment;**
- **psychological testing;**

- **secondment;**
- **employee data;**
- **redundancy;**
- **career and outplacement consultants;**
- **employee involvement and participation;**
- **equal opportunities.**

IPD MEMBERS MUST RESPECT THE FOLLOWING STANDARDS

Accuracy

They must maintain high standards of accuracy in the information and advice they provide to employers and employees.

Confidentiality

They must respect their employer's legitimate needs for confidentiality and ensure that all personnel information remains private.

Counselling

They must be prepared to act as counsellors to individual employees, pensioners and dependants or to refer them, where appropriate, to other professions or helping agencies.

Developing others

They must encourage self-development and seek to achieve the fullest possible development of employees in the service of present and future organisation needs.

Equal opportunities

They must promote fair, non-discriminatory employment practices.

Fair dealing

They must maintain fair and reasonable standards in their treatment of individuals.

Self-development

They must seek continuously to improve their performance and update their skills and knowledge.

Source: The Institute of Personnel and Development Code of Professional Conduct– codes of practice.

These IPD standards and ethics are demanding on the integrity of organisations and individuals, but there is no excuse in the normal course of events for failing to observe them.

The success of a business depends very much on getting the right person in each job. It is important that expertise and experience should be deployed to achieve it. Any one of the methods or techniques we have examined for this purpose is not guaranteed to produce successful appointments. Therefore, the wise firm will gather information by a variety of means, from application forms to testing, and weigh the evidence very carefully against the person specification before arriving at its decision to appoint. Better still, it will move towards a full assessment centre process.

PORTFOLIO ASSIGNMENT

INTERVIEW SKILLS SIMULATION

In this activity, you will experience the whole process of selecting the most suitable candidate for a job. It is a group exercise which involves simulating a job interview. Some of you will play the interviewers, some the candidates.

At the end of the session you will:

(a) be able to examine and understand role-play briefs;
(b) from the briefs, understand the value of job descriptions, and person specifications;
(c) from the profile and application forms, plan the questions and conduct a selection interview;
(d) from the interviews, gather all the information you need to decide which candidate is most likely to do the job to standard and fit in with the work group;
(e) select the most suitable candidate and justify the decision;
(f) develop skills in listening;
(g) develop skills in role-playing.

THE SCENARIO

Gainmore Superstore is recruiting a purchasing supervisor. It is your task to fill this vacancy with a suitable candidate from a short list of three.

ORGANISING THE EXERCISE

Get your teacher to photocopy pages 59–72. These contain instruction sheets and handouts to enable you to complete the exercise. There are separate instruction sheets for interviewers, candidates and teachers. The handouts provide the background information and forms needed for you to play your various roles.

- Handout 1: Gainsmore Superstore company description and structure.
- Handout 2: Job description and person profile.
- Handout 3: Interview check list.
- Handout 4: Profile of candidate A.
- Handout 5: Profile of candidate B.
- Handout 6: Profile of candidate C.
- Handout 7: Application form.

Simulation designed by Lucy Gunn © 1995

INTERVIEW SIMULATION

Instruction sheet for interviewers

Interviewers work in groups of three.

1 **Read handout 1** about Gainmore's company description and structure. Know the company.

2 **Exercise**: You are a personnel officer at Gainmore Superstore. Make a list of your roles and responsibilities within the company.

3 **Read handout 2** giving the job description of the post your are trying to fill. Know the job.

4 **Exercise:** What characteristics do you think the ideal candidate for this position should display? Complete the person profile on handout 2. This profile is in the form of a seven point plan (see page 44).

5 **Exercise:** Prepare one or two questions for each of the seven points. These should be designed to reveal whether the candidates have these ideal characteristics.

6 **The students** role playing the job candidates should have completed their application forms. Read these application forms. This is your short list of candidates. Know the candidates.

7 **Exercise**: Identify any gaps between the information given on each application and the person profile that you need to make your decision. Prepare the questions that would gain this information.

8 **Exercise**: Determine which questions **must** be asked and which *should* be asked if there is time. Have a sheet of paper with these questions set out in the order in which you intend to ask them.

9 **During the interview**: Each person in your group of three will conduct an interview with one candidate, while the other two observe and complete an evaluation form using handout 3, the interview check list.

10 **After the interview**: As a group, make notes after each interview on how you think the interview went – are there any other questions you should have asked?

11 **Discuss the information** you have gained. From this make a single choice of the candidate you (as a group) wish to appoint. Ensure you can justify your decision.

Instruction sheet for candidates

There are three candidates for the post, so three people are required to act the different people. You will play the role assigned to you. Please read and internalise your role as an actor would a character in a play.

1 Read your individual role details (on handouts 4, 5 or 6). Know your character.

2 **Exercise:** Using this information complete the person profile on handout 2 in terms of the seven point plan to match your character.

3 Read the job description on handout 2. Know the job for which your character is being interviewed.

4 **Exercise:** Having mastered your role and understood the job, complete the application form (handout 7) extracting the relevant information from your role description.

5 **Exercise:** Write a cover letter to support the application form adding any information that you feel is not covered in the application form. Give one copy of the application form and the cover letter to each of the interview groups.

6 **Exercise:** From the information you have, prepare questions which you think you **must** be asked and questions which you *should* be asked during the interview.

7 **Exercise:** Make some notes about questions you would like to ask to help you decide if you would like to work for Gainmore Superstore.

8 **During the interview:** Only give the interviewer information for which you are asked. Do not mislead the interviewer. You may give part answers to awkward questions. If a question is asked that is not covered in the role play, answer how you feel your character would.

9 **After the interview:** Make notes about the way the interview was conducted and how it made you feel. Complete the interview check list on handout 3. Think of three good points and three points which could be improved upon.

10 Use these notes at the end of the simulation to give feedback about each interview.

Instruction sheet for teachers

Familiarise yourself with each of the handouts and the instructions for the interviewers and candidates. Photocopy the handouts so that you have the required number for all those participating in the exercise.

All characters can be female or male. Names and circumstances can be changed to suit the person playing the character. Nothing is rigid except the core experience and skills given in the brief. You should note that the roles are designed so that one candidate should appear under-qualified, one ideal and one over-qualified.

1 Divide the class into groups of three. Depending on the size of the class, one or two groups will be the candidates (one group for a class of twelve, two groups for a bigger class). Brief these students on role-playing technique. The remaining groups will be interviewers. They will prepare the interviews, but will interview one character each, while the other two are observers. While one interview is being conducted, the two observers should complete handout 7 (interview check list)

2 After all three interviews have been completed, (recommended time for each is 15-20 minutes) each group should make a decision on a suitable candidate. Each group should present its choice of candidate with a full justification for the decision.

3 After all groups have made their presentations, the role players should provide feedback to each group about 'how they felt' during the interview, mentioning any information they were not asked for, and three positive points and three points which should be improved upon. Ensure the positive feedback comes first. You may have to brief them on feedback skills.

4 If you have the facilities, you may wish to video the interviews. It is the author's view that 'public' evaluation of the video can cause unnecessary pressure. An effective alternative is to provide a copy of the video for students to view privately.

5 Finally, it is useful reinforcement if the students put together a portfolio which contains all the documentation and the process, with a dialogue of the learning that the simulation achieved.

Suggested developments:

Here are three suggestions for extending the exercise.

- Before beginning the simulation, the whole class could design an advertisment for the position to be put in the local press. This could be based upon handout 1 (for interviewers only) and handout 2. It can then be used to aid the role-players' completion of the application form and the cover letter.

INTERVIEW SIMULATION

- On completion of the feedback session, a discussion or debate could be held on the selection process. This could focus on 'what went well and what went badly during the simulation'.
- After the simulation, each individual should write a report on the process of selecting the right person for the job. The report should cover the evidence indicators as outlined in the standards and reflect what the individual has learned from the simulation.

Handouts	Interviewers: give each individual a copy	Candidates
Handout 1: Company description	✔	✗
Handout 2: Job description and person profile	✔	✔
Handout 3: Interview check list	✔	✔
Handout 4: Role play A	✗	Candidate A
Handout 5: Role play B	✗	Candidate B
Handout 6: Role play C	✗	Candidate C
Handout 7: Application forms	Once completed by candidates	To be completed by candidates and then given to each interview group

INTERVIEW SIMULATION

Handout 1

Gainmore Superstore – company description

The company

Gainmore is a well-known superstore group retailing mainly food, with strong and growing clothing, household and leisure wear sections.

Location

Gainmore has over 200 superstores in the main cities and towns throughout the UK. One of the latest stores is in Great Filburgh, Suffolk.

The market

Gainmore traded successfully during the 1980s but suffered from the recession from 1988 to 1992. After complete restructuring the group is now successful and profits are in the top quartile for this segment of the market. Our recovery is mainly due to our policy of recruiting and training high-quality staff. We encourage self-development and support any training initiatives that will improve performance. Gainmore's turnover in 1994 was £5bn.

Operations

Sales are dependent upon the quality and price of our merchandise. Our buyers are highly skilled and qualified. They constantly seek new products to enhance our range and negotiate 'partnering agreements' with suppliers. It is in our customers' best interests that we look after our suppliers, providing continuity and the best value in the high street. We encourage suppliers to improve their products and their administration continuously.

Staffing

Gainmore employs more than 30,000 people, including part-timers. Since reorganisation, we have cut head office staff by 35 per cent and reduced levels of management. Our focus is on supervisory and middle management in our stores. Each store is a profit centre and has a high degree of autonomy. Most employee promotions are from within, and career change opportunities are considered sympathetically.

Working conditions

Gainmore values its staff. Salaries are above average for the industry, there is a contributory pension scheme, a sick pay scheme, and help with relocation if you are promoted to another store. Our equal opportunities policy is among the most robust in the country and managers are required to adhere to it in all matters relating to staff and customers. All our premises are designed to be safe for staff and customers. They are light and airy, with subsidised staff canteen and rest facilities. Holidays with pay start at 20 days, plus one day for each year's service, up to 30 days per year.

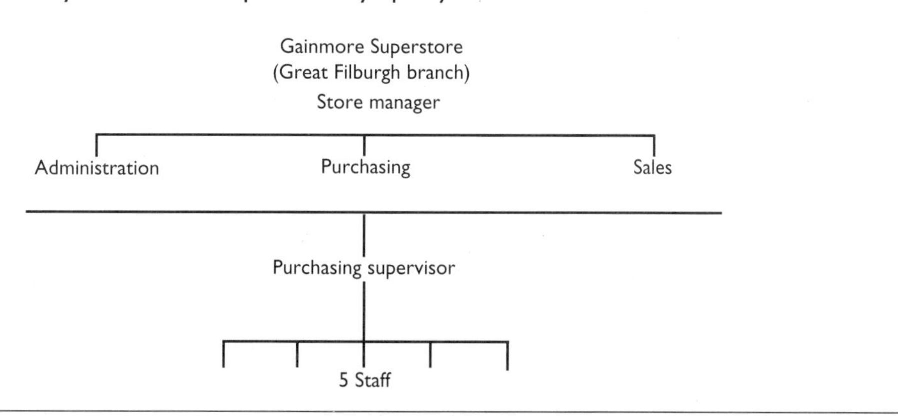

Handout 2

Job description

Job title: Purchasing supervisor
Location: Great Filburgh store
Department: Purchasing section
Answerable to: Section head

Main roles:

- to lead the work of a section dealing with the ordering, receiving and display of all fresh-food goods from local suppliers;
- to progress orders and deal with queries and matters arising from late or non-deliveries;
- to negotiate contracts with suppliers and develop partnering arrangements where appropriate;
- to liaise with customer research groups regarding range and prices of fresh fruit and vegetables;
- to maintain current records for suppliers and potential suppliers;
- to prepare monthly progress reports against milestones and report to senior management meetings on all performance and achievements;
- to constantly seek opportunities to improve performance and reduce costs.

Person profile

Job title: Purchasing supervisor

Attributes	Essential	Desirable	Disposition
Physical make-up			
Attainments			
General intelligence			
Special aptitudes			
Interests			
Disposition			
Circumstances			

Handout 3

Interview check list

Grade each of the following points 1 to 10 as follows:

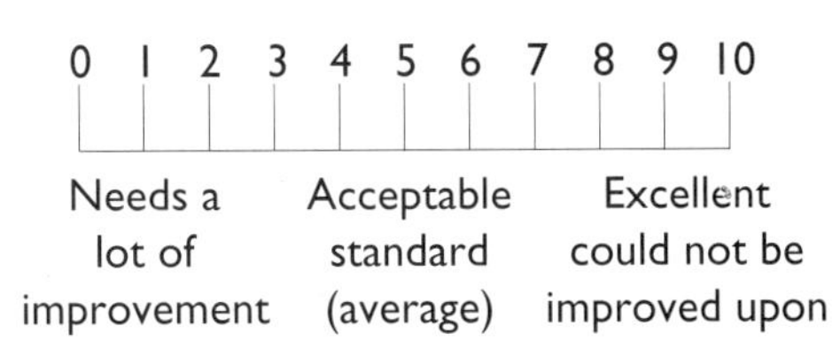

Name of interviewer

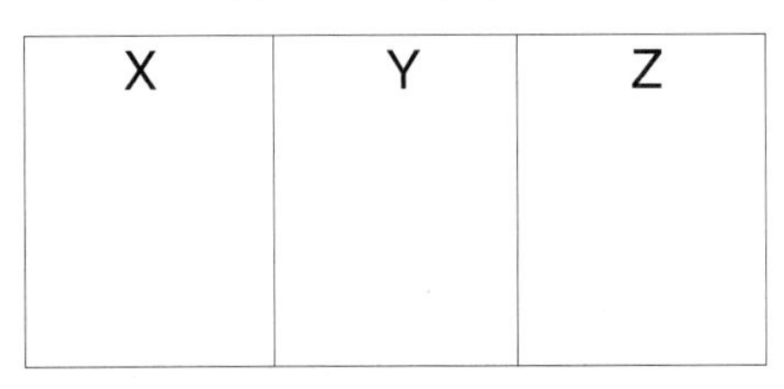

Items	X	Y	Z
Preparation: 1. Room layout/arrangement 2. All documents to hand 3. Clear knowledge of: job description personnel profile application form 4. Appropriate questions prepared for points to be investigated			

Items	X	Y	Z
Interview 5. Was applicant put at ease? 6. Was 'purpose' clearly explained? 7. Was 'structure' clear? 8. Talk ratio? Applicant? % 9. Did interview follow a pattern? 10. Use of open questions? 11. Were issues 'followed up'? 12. Were 'gaps' in history investigated? 13. Any long digressions? 14. Brisk tempo? (Business like?) 15. Clear summary? 16. Notes taken unobtrusively?			

INTERVIEW SIMULATION

Handout 4

Candidate A

Background
Born 23 March 1966 at Acle, Norfolk. Only child. Father (now dead) was a farm labourer. Mother still lives in Acle and works for local auctioneer at Acle market.

Education
Acle Junior School then Acle High. Left in April 1982 without any qualifications, due to poor health.

Health
You were found to have a spot on your lung as a result of a TB screening at school in April 1982 just as you were preparing for four O-levels and four CSEs. You spent two months in hospital and another six months receiving treatment before being pronounced fit to start work in January 1983. Doctors say you are 100 per cent fit and you feel great.

Career
You did not return to school but were lucky to get a trainee post at a new general store in the village. Because it was a small company you gained experience at just about everything, including ordering stock and dealing with suppliers and customers. You enjoyed the selling, but you much preferred the administration.

In 1987, because of the competition from big national supermarkets, you were made redundant. You saw this disappointment as an opportunity and applied for the position of purchasing officer for a wholesale fruit and vegetable merchant in nearby Filburgh.

Keen to improve yourself, you started evening classes at the College of Further Education in accounting in September 1987 and since then you have continued to do a subject a year. This year's subject is microcomputers; you are enjoying it very much and you are good at it.

You like your current work – processing orders, liaising with suppliers, contractors and your own staff. However, new technology has made it possible to organise central purchasing from the Covent Garden office, and the Filburgh office is being phased out. You have been offered a bigger job in London, but for family reasons you decline.

Domestic
You married in 1989. Your son, Brian, was born 13 months ago. You'd like a girl in about 12 months time. Your three-bedroom semi in Blobton is to your liking. It cost £39,500 in 1990 and you have a 95 per cent mortgage. All you need now is a little car and that is high on your list of priorities.

Interests
You make brass rubbings in local churches, travelling by bus and bike to towns and villages within a twenty-mile radius. You have given many away to friends and relatives for birthdays and Christmas presents. You are also secretary of the local sport and fitness club, and play for them regularly.

Disposition
You are a calm, persistent person, not brilliant, but hard-working, probably a late developer. You know what you want to do and you have a clear idea of how you are going to do it.

Present salary
£15,000. You have to give four weeks notice.

Handout 5

Candidate B

Background

Born 12 November 1969 at Thetford. You have one older sister (married to a bus driver with two children) and a younger brother (at Sussex University reading business sciences). Your parents are divorced. Your father, an area sales manager for a national firm of stationers, left home when you were nearly 15 and has never re-married. You see little of him. Your mother has a good job as manager of a ladies fashion shop in Filburgh. You now live with her in a nice house at Ellford, ten miles west of Filburgh.

Education

You left school in 1986 with three O-level passes out of six subjects taken. You believe you could have done better but the break-up of your parents' marriage undoubtedly had a disturbing effect on you.

Health

No problems of any sort since birth.

Career

Your O-levels got you into Barclays Bank as a junior and, subsequently, as a junior cashier. You studied at Great Filburgh College of Further Education for your Institute of Bankers, Part I (BTEC national certificate), but you failed one of the first year's subjects. You intended to retake it at the end of the second year but by June 1988, you were becoming disillusioned with banking as a career. Progress seemed too slow and the money was poor until you reached some of the higher grades.

So you decided to make the break. You watched the local papers for some sort of administration job with good prospects and you applied for the post of purchasing and supplies assistant in the direct works department of Great Filburgh Borough Council. You were successful and started on 1 June 1988. The direct works department is the central purchasing agency and your work has been concerned with issuing tender forms and processing of tenders for supplies and services for education, welfare, parks and gardens and corporation departments. You are in regular contact with all departments in writing and over the telephone.

You answer direct to the purchasing officer and have become very knowledgeable about the standards of service and the reliability of different suppliers. Success in this job requires thorough knowledge and understanding of procedures and familiarity with the organisation of a local government department. Both your boss and you feel you have these qualities.

You get through more work than most of your colleagues, some of whom seem to do no more than they have to. You get pretty angry about this and you don't mind showing it. The boss recognises your competence, he has delegated responsibility for handling some of his correspondence to you. You enjoy drafting letters and you take a pride in expressing yourself clearly and in good English.

INTERVIEW SIMULATION

You have enjoyed working for the council but, now that you've mastered the job, it seems not to have sufficient scope for initiative. You would now like some supervisory responsibility and the opportunity for advancement. The advertisement by Gainmore in the local paper could be the very place for you.

Domestic

You are very happy living at home with your mother. You get on well together and you live well. You have many friends, but you have no thoughts of marriage at this stage. Your seven-year-old Mini gives you plenty of freedom.

Interests

You are keen on pop music and have taught yourself to play the keyboards tolerably well. You really enjoy musical evenings at home and in your friends' houses. You have recently joined the Young Liberals, more because two of your friends are keen members than through any deep-felt political conviction. However, you have enjoyed the meetings so much that you intend to develop a more active role and become more involved with the party.

Present salary

£14,100. You must give one week's notice.

Handout 6

Candidate C

Background

Born 17 June 1953 in London where your father owned a small glazing company at Clapham. Your three older brothers are still directly or indirectly involved with the family business but you chose not to follow in their paths. Your parents recently retired and enjoy life in a quiet village in Cambridgeshire.

Education

Left school in 1969 with 8 O-levels. You could have stayed on for A-levels but you did not want an academic career – you much prefer a more business-oriented approach so you went to technical college and studied for a diploma (OND) in business studies which you passed with credits in 1971.

Career

Jobs were easy to find and you were well qualified; so you chose an appointment as a management trainee with Freeman's Mail Order near Stockwell. After two years serving in different departments following a planned programme of training and development, you were appointed supervisor – credit sanction section. You were responsible for the work of ten employees who scrutinised record cards, determined the state of the customers' accounts and decided whether they could be permitted to purchase more items on credit. It was as a result of your feasibility study that this procedure was later computerised.

In 1974, you were promoted to a 'plum' job – manager, customer relations department. You managed two supervisors each looking after eight highly-trained keyboard operators. They handled all complaints and queries from customers, using a series of standard letters which you had devised. You monitored all complaints and enquiries and produced statistics which were used in deciding which products should stay in the catalogue, which should be deleted and which should be added. The quality of your work, plus the in-depth knowledge you had gained from this job, resulted in your being promoted to assist the director of purchasing in 1981. This put you into the senior management bracket, with a company car, expense account and a 'comfortable' salary.

Sadly, within six years, your partner's health began to fail. The diagnosis was multiple sclerosis (MS) you felt you needed to spend more time together. Your partner had expressed a wish to live by the sea, and you decided to abandon your career and move out of London. Through a job agency, you applied for a job as office manager in a small food-processing factory (Lewguys) at Gorton, near Filburgh, Suffolk. Your partner was delighted and in June 1986 you moved to a bungalow overlooking the sea very near to the Lewguys factory.

You did not find the job very exciting. It was not a very efficient business and the equipment it made was very specialised. Still you set about establishing a good administration systems and took charge of all expenditure. You set up a proper purchasing system and insisted that quality controls were established so that materials were delivered according to specification and on time.

INTERVIEW SIMULATION

However, all your good work was to no avail. The company went bankrupt, and in February 1995, it closed down leaving you without a job.

Domestic

Your health is excellent but your partner's illness is taking its slow, natural course. Though confined to a wheelchair, your partner is still able to do most of the household chores including cooking. Your three children, Doris (11), Tim (9) and Alice (7) go to nearby Cliff Top School and are great kids. They help in the house and take a lot of the strain off you.

Interests

When you were busy building a career you had little time for outside interests. Now you're mainly occupied with house and family. You enjoy keeping the garden beautiful – and your partner enjoys that too. You would like to play golf but that must wait. The most important thing right now is that you get this job at Gainmore.

Present salary

Unemployment benefit, but before that you earned £10,000 at Lewguys and £17,800 at Freemans. You can start immediately.

INTERVIEW SIMULATION

Gainmore Superstore Please complete this form in black ink or typescript	Vacancies for which you wish to apply. Job function(s) Location(s)
First names (BLOCK LETTERS)	Surname (Dr, Mr, Mrs, Miss, Ms) (BLOCK LETTERS)
Address (BLOCK LETTERS) Postcode Telephone	Date of Birth Age Country of Birth Nationality
Secondary/Further Education From To Name(s) of School(s)/College(s)	Subject/courses studied and level (GCSE, GNVQ, O, A, AS, BTEC). Give examination results with grades and dates.

Any other qualifications of relevance to the position being applied for?

Work Experience: Name of Employer From To	Type of Work and main responsibilities

INTERVIEW SIMULATION

Which parts of your work experience were most beneficial to you and why?

Activities and interests.
Give details of your main activities outside work and interests to date. What have you contributed and what have you got out of them? Mention any posts of responsibility.

Explain what attracts you about the type of work for which you are applying and offer evidence of your suitability.

References.
Give the names of two references, one academic and one from your previous employment.

1. 2.

✓ MULTIPLE CHOICE QUESTIONS

1 Which of the following statements about the contract of employment are true:

A it must be in writing and handed to the employee when joining the company

B it is made up of express and implied terms

C it includes common law rights

D it must be recognised with trade unions

2 Assuming that all the employees have been employed by the employer for longer than two years, dismissal may be considered 'fair' in which of the following cases:

A the employee is not capable of doing the job he or she was employed to do

B the employee became pregnant despite being told that she might lose her job because of it

C the employees were caught sleeping whilst on duty in the security gatehouse

D the employee was found to be a member of a militant socialist group

3 Which of the following statements are false:

A trade unions are made up of manual workers who want to protect their rights

B an employer can refuse to recognise any trade union

C an employer can insist that all employees belong to the same trade union

D when a disagreement with an employer arises, a trade union must approach ACAS to negotiate with employers on its behalf

4 Which of the following management actions might gain employee co-operation:

A improving the 'payment by results' system so that those producing most earn most

B giving supervisors more authority to 'get the job done'

C making jobs as simple as possible so that people can do them without thinking

D using better lighting and background music to make the environment pleasant to work in

5 Which of the following statements describe management activities:

A an engineer designing the engine for a unique new motor car

B an accountant arranging training for her staff in the use of a new budgetary control system

C a supervisor examining the monthly lateness and absentee records for his department

D a secretary booking flights and accommodation for his director

6 Which of the following are reasons why businesses must make changes:

A to meet environmental standards

B to keep full employment

C to ensure low inflation

D to improve return on capital invested

✓ MULTIPLE CHOICE QUESTIONS

7 Which of the following are reasons that people fear and/or resist change at work:

A because they need their wages

B because they do not like shareholders taking more money out of the business

C because their trade union recommends action against it

D because they do not want to lose the use of their skills, and have to learn new ones

8 Which of the following actions helps to reduce resistance to change:

A be careful to keep everything 'confidential' until the plans are completed and then make the announcement

B choose the best people to implement the change, brief them well, and let others take redundancy

C be open about the change, and, where possible, invite participation in decision making

D be careful to prepare answers to the question 'how will it affect me?'

9 Which of the following outcomes are likely results of having employees who lack competence in their jobs:

A customers may complain about poor quality

B scrap costs may be higher

C morale may be low

D it may be difficult to recruit good staff

10 Which of the following purposes are uses for job descriptions:

A designing training programmes

B calculating wage rates

C writing job advertisements

D implementing disciplinary actions

11 Which of the following approaches might be illegal when selecting a candidate for a job as a computer programmer:

A using only male interviewers

B insisting that 'Oxford' English is spoken

C requiring specified qualifications and experience in computer programming

D requiring an ability to work on one's own

12 Which of the following Acts of Parliament should be taken into account when writing job advertisements:

A Employment Protection (Consolidation) Act 1978

B Health and Safety at Work Act 1974

C Race Relations Act 1976

D Sex Discrimination Act 1975

✓ MULTIPLE CHOICE QUESTIONS

13 Which of the following distinguishes between a job application form and a curriculum vitae (CV):

A a CV contains the personal details of the applicant

B a job application form contains details of education and experience

C a CV is initiated and prepared by the applicant

D a job application form is part of the contract of employment of the successful candidate

14 Which of the following statements about interviewing skills are true:

A interviewers seldom change their first impressions of a candidate

B to get respect, interviewers must show that they are in charge

C interviewers should look thoroughly for reasons why a candidate is not suitable for the job

D interviewers should plan to let the candidate do most of the talking

15 Which of the following statements are false:

A using tests is the safest way for managers to be certain that potential new employees will be able to do the job

B tests give additional information that can help the interviewer arrive at a decision

C personality tests will show whether a candidate is telling the truth during the subsequent interview

D tests have to be valid and reliable before they are useful predictors

16 Which of the following statements are true:

A assessment centres reduce the likelihood of selection errors

B references should be used as an opportunity to warn a future employer of a candidate's weaknesses

C ethics are a matter for personal judgement

D a business will be only as successful as the quality of its staff allows

Index